HIS TO LOVE

ELENA H. COVENS

A NOTE FROM THE NARRATOR

What I am about to tell you is completely true. However, a bit of imagination is required on your end, dear reader.

Our story follows an ordinary girl who is seemingly insignificant and unremarkable until she is unexpectedly swept away on a grand adventure filled with thievery, piracy, and all-around impropriety.

In books, much as in your own life, each action and choice you make also comes with a lesson to be learned. It just so happens that love and heartbreak go hand in hand.

However, before I tell you this tale I must ask, do you believe in second chances?

PROLOGUE

1842

Angus Underwood knew the risks of sailing into the sea, but this trip was meant to be his last before he finally hung up his hat to stay home with his family. He told himself it would be one last grand adventure. If only he knew how right he was.

You see, dear reader, the sea can be a dangerous place. Yet it is also one of the most diverse and important ecosystems to exist. It takes but it also gives. And as the waves of the ocean slammed fiercely against his ship, a fear began to take root in his heart that this truly would be his last adventure. Only this time there would be no going home.

"Captain! The ship won't hold much longer!" One of the crew members yelled as he stood in the doorway of the Captain's Cabin. "We have to turn back!"

"Not yet! If we turn back now, we will be ruined. We have families to protect. We can get through the storm. Keep going! We can break through if we push!" the captain yelled.

The boat rocked viciously as the waves slammed against the sides.

"Captain, if we don't turn back, we will die!"

The next wave hit the boat with more force, knocking both the men off their feet. Books from behind the captain spilled off their shelves and onto the floor beside him. As if to mock him, a book about sailing fell next to his face. One that was meant as a gift for his daughter.

The captain took a deep, ragged breath and closed his eyes. "Please," he begged whoever was listening, "bring me back to my daughter."

A final wave hit the ship and within seconds their bodies were weightless as the ship capsized.

AN ARRANGED MARRIAGE

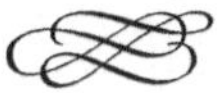

LONDON 1852

Emily

"Emily," her mother began with the same pleading tone she had used each time Emily turned down another one of her mother's invitations to a dinner which would likely end with a discussion regarding her future marriage to Lord Brimsby. "You cannot keep spending your days locked away in that old library. Heavens, they ought to tear it down by now. I swear you are the only person I ever see going in or out of that place."

In truth, Lord Brimsby was a good candidate for marriage, or so her mother told her. He was the third grandson of the Duke of Norwich. Who, according to the local word, recently gifted Lord Brimsby a townhouse which he had apparently rejected as he thought it was too small. That only made Emily less inclined to meet him. If he could scoff at a townhouse for being too small, what else could he find imperfections in?

She had heard the women whispering about his rather

"

eccentric personality. Not to mention his age. He had to have been at least twice her own age.

Emily sighed as she put on her long coat, which hung loosely around her slim figure. She pulled her auburn hair, which was a stark contrast to her pale skin and green eyes, out from under the garment. She tied it back in a bun as she glanced at her mother, Mrs. Underwood, who was the epitome of propriety.

Anyone passing Mrs. Underwood on the street would assume she was on her way to afternoon tea with one of the nobles. They were not nobility themselves, just close to it. Emily was fortunate to be born into a family that had more than enough generational money to live comfortably. It was what allowed her father to pursue his adventures before he passed.

Among the words often used to describe Emily's mother were elegant and sophisticated. Her golden hair peppered with strands of grey was never out of place, her lipstick was an unchanging shade of mulberry red, and her dresses always stretched from her collar bones down to the floor boards of Emily's late father's house. *Her* house. Though, it hardly felt like home with her mother's constant attempts to marry her off to Lord Brimsby, because heaven forbid, she want to see the world or have an adventure of her own.

"That is not true, Mother," she started, "Ms. Lewis is at the library every day making sure all of the books are in the best condition. She has spent her life with books and is perfectly happy."

Her mother let out a scoff as she shook her head slightly. "Ms. Lewis has not seen the light of day in years, she is hardly an example of a proper woman, nor is she one you should be spending all your time with. Lord Brimsby is a good man, should you just give him a chance—"

"You could have a proper life and a good family and children of your own," Emily finished in the same mocking, yet serious tone of her mother. "Yes, and as I have said I have no interest in being a wife to some lord who still thinks it is unsuitable for a woman to have her own mind. I want adventure, Mother," she pleaded. "I want to see the world. I want to meet people—real people—just like Father did."

"And where did all of his adventuring get him? Lost at sea. I am getting older, my love. I will not be here forever. It is my job to ensure you are taken care of, and I cannot do so if you refuse to even meet with him." She paused as she looked down at her gold wedding band, twisting it on her finger for a moment before her eyes met Emily's once more. "I am not saying you must marry tomorrow. Just give him a chance."

She reached beside Emily to the umbrella stand and pulled out her father's black umbrella and handed it to her. "Your father has been gone for many years now. I am sorry, my love. If you do not marry, we will lose all he built for us."

After her father disappeared when she was a girl, her mother had to assume the duties of both parents. Women only recently started working, though lucky for her mother, the bank released some of the trust funds her father had set up for them. Her mother was able to fully focus on raising her. Still, most nights she could still hear her mother praying by the bedside to bring her father home.

However their time for comfort and independence was running out. If her father didn't return by the end of the month, the police would close the investigation into her father's disappearance and he would be pronounced dead. Without a living male relative to assume the property, they would lose everything.

"Fine," Emily resigned, "I will meet him tonight, but only for *one* dinner. The month is not over yet, Mother."

Emily tucked the umbrella under her arm as she leaned forward and kissed her mother on the cheek. "I will be back within a few hours," she said softly, trying to muster a smile that would put her mother's worrisome heart at ease.

"It's about to rain, be careful. You never know what a storm might bring," her mother said.

Emily nodded as she stepped outside, closing the door behind her before she started on her normal path to the library, which would no doubt be empty upon her arrival.

Perhaps her mother's warning was a subtle way of saying, "Only bad things can happen when you're alone in a storm."

If Emily had known what awaited her when she left the house, she might have stayed home, sitting by the fire and enjoying one of the many books from her father's library. Had she taken the oncoming storm as the bad omen it was, I might be telling you a much happier story.

Yet that is not what Emily did.

And this is not a joyful tale.

A PERFECT NIGHT FOR A STORM

Emily

The rain had already begun its downpour when Emily had reached the library. It was an old building with a crooked roof and bricks that had been loose for years. A sign made of splintering wood hung loosely above the doors that read, Second Chance Books. Most of the building was covered in vines, a testament to the forgotten tales within. However, despite the many passerby who disregarded the establishment as run down, Emily was there to remember. It had become a second home.

Emily entered the forgotten trove with as much joy one might think a child would have entering a toy store. Her eyes were filled with delight at the possibilities of worlds and adventures she could never hope to experience in her real life. Despite all the stories that had been well kept by Ms. Lewis, Emily found herself drawn to the same story over and over again.

A bell chimed as Emily opened the door to the dimly lit

room, shaking off the water from her hair as she took off her coat before hanging it gently on the stand next to the entry.

"Ms. Lewis!" Emily yelled with a bright smile as she walked further into the library, where each isle was dedicated to a different genre. With no one to read the books, Ms. Lewis spent most of her days dusting and repairing old book covers one by one, racing against time. "It is absolutely dreadful outside," Emily began as she came to a stop at the base of a floor-to-ceiling bookshelf. At the very top on a rolling ladder was Ms. Lewis who was finishing with her dusting for the day. "Should I make us a pot of tea?"

Ms. Lewis was only a few years older than her mother, yet her grey hair had already taken over the once black color. Her ocean blue dress fluttered around as she turned to look at Emily with a smile that made her brown eyes appear ten years younger.

"Oh, you're here!" Ms. Lewis made quick work of stepping down the ladder and landing on the floor beside Emily. "Forget the tea, I have something for you."

"And what would it be?" Emily asked.

Ms. Lewis took Emily's hand in her own with a firm grip as she led her into a hidden room that only the two of them knew about. The room was small, though it had still become something of an escape from the dreary day to day life that was London. It was also for her own safety. Although they lived on the outskirts of London, and rules were less strict, some men would still kick up a fuss to see a woman reading in a library. Not that any have ever come by.

Emily often wondered why the library was always empty, or how Ms. Lewis came to care for it in the first place. Except, any time she would ask Ms. Lewis, she would just tell Emily not to worry her heart about such things. No one ever seemed to pay any mind to the library, so the librarian often went by unnoticed by anyone other than Emily and her mother.

The room had large, ornate windows that were latched with golden locks and green walls decorated with books and golden ornaments.

"Take a look," Ms. Lewis said as she nodded her head towards the couch in the center of the room. In front of the couch was a small table and atop the table was a plain box. "Go on then," she encouraged as Emily looked at her for any hint of what might be inside.

Usually, gifts were given on birthdays or holidays, but her birthday had passed months ago and they were not close to any significant holidays.

Emily approached the table and let herself fall onto the couch. She reached for the box and carefully lifted the lid. Inside of the box was a brown book with a golden ship riding crashing waves on the cover. She ran her fingers over the book, committing the strokes of paint to memory. It was the most precious gift she had ever been given, and no words of gratitude seemed appropriate.

"Is this what I think it is?" Emily looked back at Ms. Lewis who was leaning against the door frame, smiling.

Ms. Lewis nodded. "You have read that book so many times it was starting to falling apart. I had a little help from the print shop downtown and had them repair the bindings on it. It's good as new with a special cover. I assume you're here to read it again?"

Emily opened the book to the first page and gently ran her fingers over the corner where her father's handwriting remained.

To Emily,

May you always find adventure.

"Thank you! It's perfect."

The book had been titled 'The Adventures of the Cross Bone Pirate Thief.' Ever since her father disappeared, Emily couldn't help but be drawn to the story. She knew all the characters and everything that happened within it, yet with each read she fell in love again. The story followed a man named Flynn Sawyer, a pirate who gathers a group of men to overthrow an evil king.

Upon receiving the book as her father's final gift to her, rather than any joy that would normally accompany a gift, she felt fear at the thought of damaging it. She had left her house the very next day in hopes of finding a second copy, when she happened upon Second Chance Books. When she walked in and the bell chimed, the librarian nearly fell off the ladder in surprise. Emily only then realized how unusual it might have been for a girl to have walked into such a place, though when she saw Ms. Lewis, she felt less alone in being an outlier. However, to Emily's disappointment, Ms. Lewis had never seen the book before and had no other copies. But, offered to keep it safe in a private reading room.

That is what began Emily's routine ventures to the library and how she discovered her love of reading.

"I will leave you to it," Ms. Lewis said, "just try not to stay too long today. I don't like the look of that storm coming in."

Ms. Lewis offered a parting smile before she closed the door, leaving Emily on her own to enjoy the book.

With a sense of peace washing away the stress of her current affairs, Emily pulled the book onto her lap and opened it to the middle of the story—Flynn Sawyer was sneaking through the dead of night on a small island town to commandeer a new ship which he would later use for his crew. As much as she loved beginnings, the middle was always her favorite part.

I myself have no experience in sneaking around in the dead of night, though I do know that nothing good can come of it.

Flynn silently moved through the darkness as he approached two Emerald Guards that had been doing their rounds through the streets.

Meanwhile, the rain outside the library grew louder, the glass began to rattle and the oil lanterns flickered in and out of life. Emily could not pull herself away from the story enough to notice the war raging around her. Each sentence seemed to coil around her, pulling her deeper into the pirate's story.

Flynn ducked behind a corner as the guards grew near. He began to close his eyes to focus on the sounds when a flash of light caught his attention.

Emily's focus broke for a moment as her eyes traced over the last line. She reread it, but the words did not change.

That was never there before so why now?

Her focus was finally broken as the windows burst open, causing Emily to jump to her feet. In her haste, she dropped the book on the couch and hurried to the windows to try closing them, but, the raging wind made it nearly impossible.

"Ms. Lewis!" Emily yelled, calling for help, but she couldn't hear anything over the screaming wind. She pushed harder against the window as rain began to pour into the room, soaking everything. "Ms. Lewis!" Emily cried as she looked back at her book noticing it was still open. As the wind howled again, the windows burst open, making the book's pages turn by themselves as Emily was thrown back. She barely had a moment to think before a burst of light engulfed the room.

Emily was utterly alone when the brightness appeared. And just as quickly, darkness followed, swallowing everything in its wake.

It is at this point that I, myself, would close the book if I were not in charge of telling you this story. You see, when lightning strikes incredible things can happen. Even still, do not mistake incredible for 'good' or 'happy.' Similarly, do not mistake Emily's luck to be 'good luck.' It is simply incredible luck that Emily was in the Green Room alone, reading the book that she was, when she was, at the precise time that lightning struck.

At times like these, one might think that the story would be over. That Emily lived her life buried in books and without anything overly remarkable about her. But, as luck would have it, this is where our story begins.

A SEEMINGLY IMPROBABLE SITUATION

OAKDEN 1730

Emily

Y ou are most likely already aware that the word impossible is often misused. For example, getting sent into a world of fiction is not impossible, it is improbable. Yet, the word 'impossible' was the only word Emily Underwood was able to say over and over again as she laid on the cobblestone floor of an entirely unfamiliar place.

If you've ever been lost, then you can understand the fear and anxiousness she might have been feeling in that very moment.

Emily's eyes fluttered open to the light of hundreds of stars dancing in a darkened sky, not a stormy cloud in sight. Her head pounded and she groaned as she slowly sat up. Pushing herself onto her knees, she ignored her headache and the overall soreness of the rest of her body.

Where is everyone?

Her ears rang as she glanced around. Gone was the Green Room and the comfort of her books, and along with them, gone were the usual bustling streets of London as she knew them.

"Impossible," Emily whispered as she stood up, brushing off the dirt from her once pristine dress. "I am dreaming," she stated to herself. She let her eyes wander over her new surroundings, realizing that none of what she was seeing was familiar. "Perhaps I have died?"

She ran her hands down her body to check for any cuts, scrapes, or bruises. She felt perfectly fine.

Emily's gaze fell on the unfamiliar buildings surrounding her, noting their seemingly old design. Yet, each one looked to be in well enough condition. The air around her was fresh and in the distance, she could hear the crashing of waves against stone.

Yet what caught her attention was the sound of footsteps just past the fog that had been slowly setting in. As the steps grew closer, she was able to make out the distinct figure of two guards walking in unison. Her first thought was that there could have been a performance happening nearby, it would explain the old outfits.

Before she could call for help a hand wrapped over her mouth and pulled her deep into the darkness.

Emily clawed at the hands that held her firm against the hidden figure, but the vice like grip only grew tighter.

"I would stay quiet if you would like to see another sunrise, Princess," came a deep and gravelly voice from the man holding her captive. "I am going to remove my hand, before I do, there are a few things you need to know first. One, I have a sword, two, I have no time for morals, and three, you will live and get out of this unscathed if you listen," he warned.

Sweat beaded her forehead as her heart beat rapidly against her chest.

"Nod if you understand," he ordered.

Emily swallowed as she gave a quick nod. His hand slowly lifted from her face and her breaths came in heavy and uneven. It was all she had to not shake or fall to the floor.

"Turn around, slowly, Princess," he said.

She steadied her breathing as she carefully turned and locked eyes with her captor.

His brown skin looked soft under the moonlight, and his dark eyes which seemed to hold only reproach for her, captivated her nonetheless. His shoulder-length black hair was tied back in a bun, and his white tunic was left open at the top, exposing his muscled form beneath.

He looked her up and down briefly before the sound of footsteps approached. In one swift movement, he grabbed her arm and pulled her against him so she was hidden in the shadows from the spilling moonlight that danced across the street.

They stayed like that for the span of a few heart beats until the footsteps faded into the distance.

"Now then," the man began, "I apologize for my lack of manners, but as I am sure you can imagine I would not like to alert the guards until I have already stolen it, and am long gone, yes?"

"S-stolen what? You must have me confused with someone else—"

"Your ship, of course. Unless another princess is visiting the island at the same time as the king, I doubt there are any mistakes on my part. And given my history with your father, you must excuse me if I do not bow," he said.

"Where are we...exactly?" she asked, the feeling of unease already setting in.

Emily couldn't help but notice the lack of people or carriages.

His eyes narrowed slightly, but he brushed off her question with a shrug of his shoulders as he looked around the corner to check for more guards.

"Too much ale, Princess? We are in the town of Oakden, but that shall soon change once we are on the ship, yes?"

"Oakden..." she whispered, "as in the black-market town off the Sea of Lost Souls?"

Once again, his eyes narrowed before he nodded. "Yes, that's the one," he said as he turned to look around the corner again.

"No, that's impossible, it doesn't exist," she said as she shook her head. "Alright, it's alright," she reassured herself. "I am dreaming. I was struck by lightning, and I am probably unconscious in the Green Room right now."

The man slowly turned around and looked her up and down as his mouth hung open slightly.

"Are you daft?" he finally asked. "Or are you drunk?"

"How dare you!" she gasped, momentarily forgetting his earlier threats. "I will have you know that I am perfectly sound of mind—in fact, many would argue that I have more mind than most men."

"Is that so?" he asked through a slight smirk.

"Yes."

"Well then, Princess of Sound Mind, may we leave? Because in a few moments, more guards will come from the same place that you did, and I don't make idle threats, Miss. And," he continued, "if it is as you say, that this," he lazily gestured to the scenery around them, "is all a dream, then let this be a harmless adventure where you humor a poor thief."

She didn't want to admit it to such an insolent man, even

still, he was right. Her whole life she had been wanting a grand adventure and here it was, presenting itself before her, even if it is a shock induced dream. Come morning, she would be back at home with her over concerned mother and her normal routine.

"Fine."

"Now, then, glad that is all sorted. Remember, stay silent and move quickly as I would hate for unnecessary blood to be spilled tonight."

Without offering her a moment's respite, the strange man grabbed her hand as he darted out from the alley and dashed into the fog. Emily nearly tripped as she rushed to keep up with him, pulling her dress above her feet with the other hand.

Their footsteps echoed off the stone walls as they picked up pace. It was incredible that her dreams could be so real, everything was like it had been in her book, right down to the mysterious atmosphere.

Their running came to a stop as they approached a large ship that looked to be straight out of one of her stories.

The strange man pulled her down with him to crouch behind some barrels, as he watched the two guards standing watch next to the ramp up to the ship.

"What are we doing?" she whispered.

"Shh," he hissed, holding up one finger.

Suddenly, the deafening sound of a bell tower rang through the town. In the break between the ringing, Emily could hear the guards yelling to get to the court.

"Perfect timing if I do say so myself," he said, turning his head back to offer her a toothy grin.

The two of them stood up and made their way towards the bridge, still watching for any guards that might be headed towards whatever emergency had occurred.

It was impossible, in Emily's educated opinion, that just a moment ago she was in the Green Room Ms. Lewis had constructed for her, and now she was boarding a ship with a strange man who had just threatened her life.

Even with the strangeness of it all, it was also absolutely thrilling.

"We should have enough time to get her out into the open ocean before they realize she is gone," the man said as he began making his way to the bridge of the ship where the helm was located. "Be a dear and remove the ropes that are tethered to the ship."

"I don't even know your name, you cannot just order me around like that, besides," Emily crossed her arms over her chest and raised her tone as the strange man stopped walking and turned his head over his shoulder to watch her, "what if they come back as I am untying the rope? You should give me a weapon to defend myself."

The man let out a low laugh as his sharp smile tugged at the corner of his lips. He turned around slowly and began to walk towards her, causing her to step back in time.

"You do not know me? Well...I guess your father keeps you more sheltered than I thought," he said as he took another step towards her. He nodded his head as he extended his arm in a mock-bow. "I am Captain Flynn Sawyer, the most feared pirate on this side of the world, pleasure to make your acquaintance, Princess."

"Maybe I have gone mad. You are nothing like I thought you would be. Perhaps my dreams aren't as accurate as I thought," she said.

Flynn smirked. "Ah so you know my name and not my face, yet you dream of me at night?"

Emily grimaced. "If I were to dream of a man like you, they would rather be called nightmares."

"And yet, you still think of me at night. And regarding the guards, you have no reason to fear the men coming back as I—"

"Let loose all the stable horses in the courtyard," Emily finished, "or so I assume."

Flynn's brows furrowed slightly. "Perhaps...have you been following me?"

His eyes suddenly grew wider and within a breath, he pulled his sword from his hip and pointed it at Emily's neck; she gasped as she stepped back, tripping on her own dress sending her crashing to the deck.

"Has your father really sunk so low as to use his own daughter as bait?" he spat.

Emily didn't know why she was so nervous. After all, if this was a dream, then she was trapped in her own mind, and he could not truly hurt her.

Something about Flynn, at least the Flynn in her dreams, commanded her attention. Despite this being a dream, he struck her heart with a deep fear that his earlier threat was true. He had no time for morals.

Emily could tell him that this was all a dream and there was no evil king, and even he himself was no more than words on paper mixed with her own imagination. And yet, against her better judgement, the words that came out of her mouth only seemed to pull her deeper into his world.

"I do not know who you think I am, Flynn Sawyer, but I am *not* a princess, and the only father I have ever known died when I was a young girl. And, if you want to get out of here and on the water before the guards realize that the king isn't the target of whoever let loose the rampaging horses, then I suggest you help me untie the ropes."

Flynn narrowed his eyes and reluctantly sheathed his

sword at his hip. He reached for her hand, and she accepted with as much doubt as one might expect.

"Very well then...if you are not a princess, then who are you? Oakden isn't exactly a place for women like you."

Emily scoffed. "And who exactly are women like me?"

She turned from him and began to untie the ropes that still clung to the ship, tossing them into the water. After a moment, Flynn followed suit, ridding the ropes from the boat with ease.

"Sheltered, rich parents, fair skin that hasn't known the harshness of a beating sun, expensive dresses, and soft hands, Princess," he explained as he threw the last rope into the water.

"Apparently, Oakden isn't a place for well mannered men either," she muttered under her breath. "How do you expect to man a ship with two people?"

Flynn dusted his hands off and crossed his arms over his chest. "First off, she is a double mast schooner, who's to say three dedicated bodies cannot handle her?"

"Well, I count you and me. Perhaps your time would be better spent studying than kidnapping unsuspecting women."

Flynn chuckled. "Who says I am alone, Princess?"

"What do you—"

Emily's words were cut off by the sound of footsteps coming onto the deck. She turned around and saw two men climbing aboard. One of the men with tan skin and brown hair turned and kicked the steps up to the boat off into the water. When he turned back, she could see that an eye patch covered his right eye.

The other man had light brown hair and harder features. His pale skin took on a midnight hue under the moon.

"Alright, Cap," the light brown-haired man said as he stepped forward, dropping a heavy crate onto the ground with a thunk. A clang of metal sounded from inside the box. "Let's get this mistress out on the water, it won't be long before they realize that the king—"

"Isn't the target of the rampaging horses..." Flynn finished. He looked beside him at Emily, his brows were furrowed and he seemed like he wanted to say something. But, he turned his attention back to the men.

"Ah, why yes. That is what I was going to say," the light-brown-haired man said as he stepped closer to them. The man with dark brown hair followed behind.

Both of the men came to a halt when they saw her, and the one with dark hair nodded towards Flynn.

"There is a woman on the ship," the dark-haired man said in a matter-of-fact tone.

Flynn nodded. "At least your eye does not deceive you."

"*Why* is there a woman on the ship?" he amended.

"And why is she so beautiful?" the light-haired man cooed.

Emily took a step back to stand slightly behind Flynn, but he shoved her away from him.

"It is none of your concern," Flynn grumbled. "There will be a delay in our travels. The only thing you need to know is that the goal remains the same. Lucas, set her up in the Captain's Cabin for the night. I will not be sleeping tonight. When you are done, you are to report back to me. Levi, you are to help me get us out on the water. She is small enough that we will manage on our own."

"Aye, Cap." Lucas, the dark-haired man, said. He moved forward and extended his elbow for Emily. She stared at Lucas in disbelief. He really did look exactly how she had pictured him. Emily glanced back at Flynn for reassurance, but instead he turned his back on her and strode up to the helm. "Let's go then, Miss," Lucas said, calling her attention back to him. "The night is still young so you will have plenty of time to rest," his voice was soothing, gentle even.

Emily took his arm and followed him past the mast to the door to the cabins. She gave one last look over her shoulder for Flynn, but he was already gone.

Maybe it was the way Flynn spoke to her that was such a contrast to how he spoke in the book, or maybe it was the realness of being on a commandeered ship that made Emily notice the cold feeling of dread slowly seeping into her. How could her dream feel so real? When would she wake up? Would she ever wake up? Her heart refused to settle at the thought of never being able to leave her dream-like state.

MISTAKES UPON MISTAKES

Flynn

Flynn never made mistakes. He was aware that mistakes and stupidity were what got you killed. Now, he feared, he was guilty of both. If she were to be lying and she was the king's daughter, the king would come after him with a fleet of ships before Flynn was prepared. Though, he wouldn't be coming because he feared that his precious daughter had been captured by pirates. No, he would come out of necessity to save face among his opulent patrons. It would be an embarrassment for him to have lost anything to someone much lower than himself.

On the other hand, if she was as she says, *not* the king's daughter, then he had just kidnapped a completely innocent woman.

When he found her, she had looked confused and scared. Everyone was to be in the town square to greet the king. It would have been seen as an insult not to go.

She looked lost. When he saw her on the ground, a distant part of him felt drawn to her. Hell, he didn't even know her name and yet she was on his ship resting in the Captain's Cabin...in what was supposed to be his bed.

He drummed his fingers against the helm.

Who are you?

She didn't show much fear towards him. In fact, she seemed more composed than most women upon meeting Flynn.

"So," Levi began, stepping up the stairs to join Flynn at the helm. "A woman on board? Supposed to be bad luck."

Levi was as cunning as he was superstitious. Flynn learned that early on when he refused to set sail one day because Lucas brought a banana as a snack.

"A woman on board is only bad luck if she bleeds."

"Right, well, if we get thrown into the sea to the lockers below, I will haunt you for eternity."

"You already do that. The only respite I can hope for is in my own demise."

"Seriously, Cap. Who is she? Why take a hostage?"

"She is not a hostage," Flynn corrected, his words holding more bite than he was used to. "She is..." *a hostage.* "Insurance."

"Right...and after months of planning this heist down to the smallest details, what would we need insurance for, and how is she of any value? Her clothes are of quality, sure, yet she bares no family crest or signs of importance."

This is going swimmingly.

"She *may* be the king's daughter. I found her while you two were off distracting the guards. If I didn't take her, I could have been caught and then everything would have been for nothing."

"I see," Levi said as he clapped Flynn's shoulder. "I get it. You had no choice but to kidnap the lone beautiful woman," he said, his voice drenched in sarcasm.

"She is *not* beautiful," Flynn snapped. She was just some woman who got in the way and to avoid capture, he did what was needed, he reminded himself.

"Lucas is the one with the eye patch, Cap. Your eyes work just fine. Besides, if you're wrong, and she is not the king's daughter, what's your plan?"

"I will let her go."

"That's wonderful. She can run right back to the guards and tell them everything."

"Then what would you suggest? We keep her? Having her here will only make things harder."

Levi shrugged his shoulders. "All I am saying, is that we have a lot riding on this."

"Levi is right," Lucas interjected as he joined them from below the helm. He stepped up the stairs keeping one hand on the wall beside him, until he came to stand next to Levi. "We have planned this for months. She seems just as confused as the rest of us. If she was the king's daughter, don't you think she would have more bite to her, or at least understand the gravity of the situation? Why was she even near the docks to begin with? Why was she unguarded?"

"So you believe she is just another aristocrat's spawn?" Levi asked.

"I am not claiming to think anything. In any case, we need a plan."

They were right, of course. None of this was meant to be happening. Everything they worked for, everything they sacrificed, everyone they lost at the king's hand. All of it would be for nothing because of some fair skinned, doe eyed woman.

"We will dock at Dardurin," Flynn said with as much finality in his voice as he could. "We will make a plan come morning. She doesn't know our intentions, and if she does go to the guards, they will make little effort to chase down any pirate that took her for only a day."

"You want to bring her home?" Lucas asked. He was always skeptical, logical, he never made a move without first considering all of the possible outcomes.

Flynn met Lucas's worried gaze. "Everything will still go as planned, my friend."

Lucas nodded. "Alright. If we stop at Dardurin, perhaps we can enjoy the festivities while we are there."

"And the many beautiful women that I left behind during my last visit," Levi said with a wink to Lucas.

Lucas's expression hardened as he looked away.

Flynn shook his head at his whoreish friend. "There has never been a woman you haven't wanted to fuck or a drink you have ever walked away from. You will die lonely, young, and drunk."

Levi was always quick to jump into bed with any woman who gave him a smile, and most days he was drunk. He licked his wounds rather than dealing with the cause by burying himself in one distraction or another. Even still, he was as loyal as they come. And when it came to finding his sister, he was determined. He once slept with a noble woman in order to gain a favor which he later used to get the latest trade route information. It was only later that Flynn learned she was the wife of a higher-up in the Emerald Guard.

"Correction," Levi defended. "I have never met a woman who didn't want to fuck *me*. Everyone has a price. Sex and money just happen to be languages that everyone speaks."

Lucas scoffed. "Until you open your mouth and they realize how daft you are. Then what will you do? If you ever marry, for her sake, I pray that she is deaf."

"You are just jealous, my friend," Levi said as he reached

forward to pinch Lucas' cheek which earned him a whack upside the head by the eye-patched pirate. "Because at least women think I am funny. You, on the other hand, haven't taken a woman to bed in all the years we have known each other."

"Perhaps I am just focused on the mission, unlike—"

"Enough!" Flynn yelled, turning back to look at the two men who were one more argument away from a duel. "We will deal with her come morning. If there are any objections you may bring them forward. If it is settled, then I am retiring to bed for a few hours. If you two can manage not to kill one another, or capsize the ship, it would be greatly appreciated."

"I thought you said you were taking the night shift," Levi teased.

"Changed my mind," Flynn shot back, letting Lucas take over the helm as he walked away. Away from his arguing friends and away from the woman laying in his bed. He quickly walked to the opposite end of ship until he made it below deck where the hammocks hung, swaying slighty with the movements of the boat.

Seeing his new sleeping quarters only brought on a fresh wave of frustration.

"Fucking perfect," he muttered to himself as he steadied the hammock with one hand, hoisting himself into his new bed for the night.

Once he was stable enough that he could lay down without fear of falling, he covered his face with his arm and let his body relax. The cold tendrils of guilt began to take root in his chest. He wanted to apologize, or find some way to make it right with the woman aboard the ship. Yet, his own pride made it nearly impossible.

How long had it been since he'd even had a normal

conversation with a woman? He felt out of touch, like he was to navigate a maze come morning. He always prided himself on his ability to lock everything out, stay focused, and do what needed to be done. But something in her eyes called out to him. As if she were just as lost as he was.

Perhaps she is actually a siren meant to lure me to my death.

He laughed at the idea.

Or mayhap I am the one that is daft. It is not like me to be so careless.

THREE PIRATES AND A BOTTLE
OF RUM

Emily

The motion of the ship's rocking made Emily stir from her sleep. It wasn't overly dramatic in its movements, but Emily had never been out at sea. The feeling was enough to cause her stomach to roll.

She had always wanted her father to teach her to sail, but that day had never come.

Emily stood on shaky legs and carefully walked out of the stern of the ship and up the stairs towards the deck where she could hear two men laughing.

When she stepped out onto the deck, she saw Lucas steering the ship while Levi threw back a bottle of what smelled like rum. As she took another step, the floor boards groaned under her weight.

Both men snapped their heads towards her, and their sharp features softened once they met eyes with Emily. Levi's shoulders relaxed and he gave her a grin, while Lucas offered a nod of his head as he turned his attention back to the sea.

"Ah, Princess," Levi said as he swung his arms open and gave a drunken bow. "So nice of you to join us. Did this fool's sailing wake you?" he joked as he slapped Lucas across the back.

"My sailing is perfectly fine, it was probably your half drunken stories that woke her," Lucas grumbled, yet Emily could see the corner of his mouth had perked up.

Emily chuckled as she shook her head. "Not at all, I am just not used to the sea I'm afraid."

Lucas hummed in agreement. "Well Miss, we will be back on land in no time. If you cannot sleep, would you care to join us?"

"Wouldn't that upset Flynn?" she asked. It was incredibly dark so she could be wrong, but as she looked around, she could not see him anywhere.

"Oh Cap has always had a stick up his arse if ye ask me."

This time, Lucas was sure to give Levi a smack upside the head.

"What my drunkard of a friend means to say, is that Cap is in the crew's quarters below deck, getting some shut eye until the sunrise. We won't tell if you won't, Miss."

Hearing 'Miss' instead of princess was a welcome change.

Emily looked around the ship one more time as she bit her bottom lip. She wasn't scared of Flynn, yet a part of her wanted to remain on his good side for the time being. Even if this was just a dream.

Once she was sure that they were alone, she nodded her head. "Very well then, I shall stay."

"She shall stay!" Levi exclaimed as he threw his hands up, sloshing the liquid in his bottle around, only spilling a few drops on the deck.

"What were you talking about?" she asked the two men.

"Ah," Lucas began, "we were reminiscing, Miss. About how we each found ourselves here in the first place."

"Well, I always love a good story," she said.

"Well, you're in for a treat then," Levi said as he moved closer to Emily. "Lucas has the most interesting tale of us all. Even so, perhaps I shall go first?"

Levi looked to Lucas who only waved his hand dismissively.

"I was perhaps seventeen years of age when Cap found me. He broke into the cellars the night before I was to be executed. I was on my way to the gallows. Ye see, after my parents died, I had to resort to stealing to feed my sister. She was only fifteen years old and she was sick, she needed to eat more than I did. So, I only ever stole enough for her. Well, one day, I wasn't as careful as I should have been and I was caught by the Emerald Guards. They took me and my sister. I was rotting in a cell knowing that come morning, I would be hanged. Yet the worst of it all, they never brought my sister to the cell with me. They took her to the King's Palace. But all I could do was watch and wait for my own death. That is when Cap found me. Asked me to be a member of his crew. He promised me that if I stuck with him, he would kill the king and I would get my sister back."

"So you have been searching for her this whole time? I never knew..."

Levi barked a laugh. "Well, how could you? We only just met."

"Ah...yes. My apologies."

"It hasn't been all bad," Levi said. "I learned how to be silent with the Cap's help. Now I can rob a person blind without them knowing I was ever there. They call me the Ghost."

Levi dramatically waved his hands about, imitating a ghost.

"If only he were always silent," Lucas said. "No one calls you the Ghost. 'Sides, we never stay in one place long enough for you to gain a nickname."

"Maybe it's you with the stick up the arse," Levi mumbled as he threw his bottle back and took another sip.

"Well, one of us has to stay focused. We each have a reason for being here, we cannot afford to forget that." Lucas offered a warm smile to Emily.

"And what's your story, Lucas?" she asked.

"I was in the business of acquisitions and contracts, Miss."

Levi choked on his next swig of rum, bending forward to cough. Emily rushed to slap his back. She almost laughed at his answer. The book only touched on it slightly, but Lucas was certainly not a business man. After a brief coughing fit, Levi stood up and wiped the alcohol from his lips.

"What this self-righteous prick means to say, is that he was a gun for hire. Come on now, *Mr. Acquisition*, tell her the actual story."

Lucas sighed. "Years ago, when I was a boy, I was in an orphanage. I was well beyond the age of ever having hope of being adopted, so I felt like I had to study. If I could not get a decent life handed to me like so many had, I would earn it myself. I would study and learn everything there was to learn. However," he paused, looking at Emily. His gaze didn't hold anger or hurt as he looked at her dress. His expression was soft and he pursed his lips for a second before turning back to the water. "When one has no money or family name to help get by, sometimes thievery is the only way to get what you need."

She examined her dress. She had never thought much of

it before, but her clothes were always of fair quality. She had never gone without a meal or without knowing if she would have a roof over her head the next day.

She was suddenly all too aware of how she must have come off to the men she was *acquired* by.

"So you are a thief like Levi?" she questioned.

"Ah, no, Miss. I have to admit, I got caught my first time stealing. I knew I needed books, but I couldn't afford to buy one. There was a library in an older, well off, gentleman's house. This much I knew from his maids. They would often gossip after work near the tavern. So one night, I crept into his house to steal a few books. I had every intention of returning them, I just needed to learn how to read first. Then I would put them right back where I found them. Or that is what I told myself. But I didn't make it out of his house that night. He stopped me by the door and demanded to know what gold or jewels I was stealing. When I showed that it was only books, he asked, 'Why? Why only take books when I have more riches than I know what to do with?' So I told him everything. He offered me a deal. He would teach me everything he knew, teach me to read and think, teach me how to rub elbows with the higher class. I would become his son. In exchange, I would work for him in his business."

"Killing people? You were just a boy," Emily said.

"Aye, I was. Still, he trained me. Cared for me, and kept to his word and taught me. I became one of the best assassins under his order. And he became like a father to me."

Levi leaned closer to Emily. "It is how he got such an aristocratic last name."

Lucas smiled softly. "I took on my father's last name, Sinclair. Having an opulent last name is better than having no last name at all."

Levi chuckled, taking another swig of the rum.

"So then," Emily continued, "if you were happy, what led you here?"

Levi had also quieted down, just as eager to hear the next words.

"Word of my skills quickly traveled. I could blend in with anyone and yet I was no one. He kept my identity close to the heart, never telling anyone who I really was. Still, I knew everything that he did. I became somewhat of an insurance policy for him. Well, turns out word of my ability traveled much higher than I knew at the time. One of the Emerald Guards came to see my father. I was there visiting and my father ordered me to hide in the wardrobe and to not come out. The guard asked if he knew anything, but he refused to answer. Told the guard that he was simply a business man through and through. The guard killed him where he stood. His empire fell with him. It was at the funeral that Cap found me. Offered me much the same as Levi." He lifted his coat with a hand and pulled out a golden pistol, waving it in the air for Emily to see. "I took my father's pistol, with only a bullet left, and told Cap that I would join him if he let me be the one to deal the final blow."

"So both of you have been hunting the king, then?"

"That depends," Lucas responded.

"On what?"

Levi leaned over so he was right beside Emily, the smell of rum permeating the air. "On whose side yer on."

Emily felt her heart stop in her chest, the atmosphere seemed to change as both the men stared at her. Her eyes danced between the two pirates.

"I-I am not the princess, if you would listen, I could explain and you will see that this has all been a huge misunderstanding—"

Lucas held up his hand for her to be quiet and she closed her mouth, keeping her eyes on him. "There is one story that hasn't been told. The story of how Flynn became as deadly a pirate as he is."

Levi took one last sip from his bottle before setting it down on the floor. "No one becomes a feared pirate without first giving people a reason to be feared," he started. "We do not care if you are or are not a princess. It matters little. And besides, it's not like you can betray us. You'll be sent to the gallows right along with us."

"Why would I be sent to the gallows? I have done nothing wrong," not that she should have been overly concerned, Emily reminded herself.

"Well, Miss, did you help commandeer a ship?" Lucas asked.

"Yes."

"And did you ask for a weapon to fight against the guards?" Levi questioned.

"Yes...I did."

Levi looked at Lucas who only smirked slightly. "Well then, princess or not a princess, I believe that makes you a pirate right along with us. So as the code goes!" Levi said as he jumped towards Lucas and swung his arm around his friend. "Drink today, burn tonight, and may we live for one more fight!"

Lucas laughed as Levi chanted his code.

Emily felt herself relax as she released a breath she didn't know she held. Both the men seemed at ease with her being on the ship, but their warning was not missed. If she were to become a problem, they would not stand in the way to help her.

Flynn spoke up from across the ship, silencing any hollers or chants that the men had been screaming. "And if you should see the gallows come sunrise, may your cause be immortalized."

Both Levi and Lucas quieted down as their captain started towards them. Levi let his arm drop from Lucas as he reached down to pick up his bottle, tossing it at Flynn.

Flynn caught the bottle by the neck and gave it a quick shake, measuring how much was left. Once he seemed satisfied, he tipped it back, taking a sip as he kept his eyes on Emily.

She felt her face redden under his heated gaze. Once he was done, he lowered the bottle to hang beside him.

"Never forget that last part," Flynn said. "What we do, what we fight for, will always lead back to the gallows should we ever be caught. Now," he said, glancing between the three of them. "Go get some rest. I will take over the helm. A few more hours till we dock."

"Aye, Cap," the men said in unison, quickly making their way past Emily and Flynn towards the crew's quarters.

Emily waited until the men disappeared below deck before she brought her attention back to Flynn. His jaw was hard set and his shoulders were stiff as he took over Lucas' position.

"So what is your story? How did you become the great Flynn Sawyer, Feared by all?" she asked. She stood across from him, leaning against the wooden rails.

Flynn didn't respond. The only sign that he heard her was the tightening of his grip on the helm.

"Well then," she said, clasping her hands together in front of her as she started to head back to the Captain's Quarters. "It is getting late. I will leave you to all your... pirating and brooding."

"I am *not* brooding," he grumbled.

"Of course, you aren't. My mistake. I thought I saw a miserable looking man, drinking by himself."

Flynn sighed. "Stay."

It wasn't a question.

"Are you afraid of the dark?" she quipped.

"Any man with half his mind would be wise to be afraid of the dark. Still, you will stay so that I may keep an eye on you."

"We are out at sea!" she said, pointing to the darkness around them. "What trouble could I possibly get into? Besides, I am tired. I want to sleep."

And try to wake up from this dream.

"I don't know, but I do not want to find out. You can rest when we dock. Won't be long now."

Emily muttered a few curses under her breath and he *smirked*. The very idea of that dastardly pirate finding any humor in her discomfort only encouraged the need to argue. Yet, she also knew Flynn—at least from her books— well enough to understand that he was more stubborn than a mule.

She threw her hands up and walked back towards him, sitting down at his feet with a sigh. Emily needed to sleep. Once she was able to get to sleep, she was sure that she would wake up from this dreadful dream. However, Emily also had to give her own imagination credit. Everything about her dream had been so real. The coldness of the wind on her skin, the feel of the wood of the ship, none of it felt faint or indistinct like it would in a dream.

Even Lucas and Levi were here. Though, if this were the book, Lucas would also be above deck aiding in manning the ship, not in the sleeping quarters below deck.

Her mind raced to come up with an explanation as to why she would have such a realistic dream. After all, when one is forced into a situation that doesn't make sense, one's brain will create stories or other matters of fiction to bring reason to the unreasonable.

For example, I would bet that sometimes you stay up at night looking at your door that you left open, just a crack, staring at a hung sweater. But, if you stare too long, it might take on the shape of a person and appear as if it was moving.

It is this very method of explanation that allowed Emily to believe she was in a dream, and not on a boat setting sail to collect a band of dangerous men, from an even more dangerous location; Butchers Harbor.

I myself would be in no hurry to visit any location with a name like that.

But as Emily is silently telling herself right now, this is just a dream, and it is also just a story.

MISTAKEN IDENTITY

Emily

We have all had the misfortune of calling out the wrong name, or maybe saying hello to a stranger on the street that you thought looked like someone you know.

Though, unless you have made the grave mistake of kidnapping the wrong person before, or worse—being kidnapped and accused of things you have not done, then this situation might seem easily solvable by clearing the air and taking a moment for introductions.

But when the person who kidnapped you is your favorite character from a book you have read countless times, they might think you are out of your mind.

If Emily hadn't read this book as many times as she had, she might have had more questions floating about her mind as she leaned against the wall of the ship, looking out into the crashing waves, which were painted with strokes of white from the moonlight above them.

As Emily looked out at the myriad of blues and whites,

she thought about her predicament. It was strange, everything felt so real. She held out her hand in front of her. The cold sea water spraying her fingertips as she recalled the sensation of Flynn pulling her along, his rough hands wrapped around hers. It was more true to life than any dream she had ever had before.

It was as if she had been transported into his world...

Emily cast the preposterous idea out of her mind as she brought her arm back within the ship and searched for the source of her recent frustrations.

She angled her head to look at the helm of the ship where Flynn, or at least her version of him, stood. He controlled the boat with ease, occasionally looking down at his golden compass while Levi and Lucas rested below deck.

For a brief moment, Flynn glanced towards her before looking back at the ocean beyond her.

"We will dock soon at a quiet town. We will spend the night at an inn. From there, you should be able to catch the next boat back," he said as he ignored her stare.

"What do you mean?" she asked. "I thought we were setting sail to—" she paused. How much could she really tell him? Even if this was a dream, she could disrupt his course if she said too much. So far, they have remained consistent with the book, aside from a few minor details. But, how far could she allow them to stray from the plot before spelling disaster? What effect, if any, would their story have on her waking up? "To somewhere else?" she finished.

Once again, his reproachful gaze met her curious one.

After a moment he shook his head. "It is too late to turn back. I will let you off at the next port so you may catch safe passage back to Oakden, where you may then alert the guards of the *'pirate scum'* that held you captive. I will give you enough coin to get back."

"All of a sudden you are offering to help me?" she asked, leaving the side of the boat where she had been enjoying the moonlight. Flynn watched as she approached, taking his eyes off her to look at the vast sea or down at his compass.

Emily stepped up to stand beside the helm. She looked down at the compass in his hand and could see the initials H.S. engraved on the inside. Before she could ask Flynn to tell her about it, he cleared his throat. She looked up at him and instantly met his eyes. Flynn's gaze held so much anger within it as if he was truly suffering.

"Despite what you may think, Princess," he began in a rough but even voice, "I do not make a habit of kidnapping innocent women. I understand the scare you might have had, so at the very least I will offer you assistance in getting home."

"Who says I was scared? I was taken by a man who claimed to be a captain yet he had no ship. I was beginning to think you were a man playing dress up. You don't even have a pistol."

Flynn chuckled. "First of all," he began, "a sword is a gentleman's weapon. And secondly, not all of us are born into lives of luxury, Princess. Some of us have no choice but to resort to thievery, especially if the end outweighs the means."

"And what end would that be?"

He hesitated for a moment. He looked down at the compass as his thumb rubbed the swirling pattern on the side.

"I see...an end where people can be free. We live in a world that punishes the poor through taxation with little improvement despite the many promises that are given, and rewards the rich for their cruelty to those below them. To escape this end, any means by which this is achieved is acceptable."

"So, you are for the people and for the downfall of those who create this world?" she asked, though, she already knew the answer. In reality, their worlds did not seem all that different. Emily was no fool. She knew she led a privileged life, but she also knew about the horrors that existed outside of the safety her mother had created for her.

"Well, the rich have more than enough to share," he said with a sly smirk. "I am simply helping them in doing so."

"Oh my apologies, then," she bowed. "I had no idea I was being kidnapped by Robin Hood himself."

Flynn's brows furrowed as he watched her carefully, his lips still teasing at a smirk. "I do not know this man, but I am sure that is not a compliment."

"You could only wish to be half the thief he was, he had a moral code. Steal from the rich and give to the poor. You, on the other hand, commandeered a ship and kidnapped the *wrong* woman. You are doing a mighty job at being a captain," she said as she spun on her heel and began to walk away from him. Flynn grabbed her arm before she could escape his reach and pulled her back towards him, so she was only a breath away from him.

"I do have honorable intentions, Princess. Whichever way I intend to achieve this future, with whatever means I see fit, they are not of your concern. You may think me to be pirate scum, but I am not. Not all of us get to choose the role we are thrown into, Princess. One cannot always follow the law when doing a good thing, because the law is never capable of creating change."

Her breath hitched at their closeness. "What do you mean?"

"When the law is just, the evil is too powerful. When the law is unjust, the people are powerless. Either way, no one can make a difference obeying the law."

Emily swallowed as her eyes darted between his before dropping his gaze. "Then, let us start over, Flynn Sawyer. It seems as if we have both made ill judgments against one another. You keep calling me a princess, but I have told you that I am not."

"No, you are not *my* princess, but," he paused as he let his eyes roam down her form, examining her clothing, "you must either be *a* princess or a marvelous thief if you are wearing such expensive clothes. Tell me, who are you?"

I have always thought that the question 'who are you' was interesting. It could mean what hobbies do you have, how would you define yourself as different from everyone else, what is your name, or in this case, are you in any way related to the royals that have supported the very king your captor intends to lead a mutiny against.

Also in this case, Emily knew that much of who she was would be nonsensical to him. London didn't exist within the pages of the book, and to say that she was simply a plain girl with a plain name and a penchant for reading books of grand adventures, specifically *his* book, would only raise more questions than it was worth.

"I," she began, her mouth opened and closed briefly as she searched for an appropriate answer. "I am no one really —or what I mean to say is that I am not a princess, I am just a girl from...nowhere," she searched his eyes for any sign that he would believe her. What she said was not a complete lie after all.

"Nowhere must mean somewhere," he mused. "What? Do you have a rich controlling father you are running from or perhaps a deep dark secret of your own that you are harboring?"

"No secrets. Besides, why would I tell my captor anything about myself?"

He hummed quietly as if examining her answer before he nodded his head. "Well, we are all from nowhere I suppose, trying to get to somewhere together," he said in a hushed tone. For the first time since their disastrous meeting, Emily felt like she understood his words and all the loneliness that they carried.

"Even still," he continued, slowly pulling away as he released his grip on her. Emily stumbled back, ignoring the lingering warmth in the absence of his touch. Flynn looked back up at the open waters that were mainly shrouded in darkness and nodded towards something. As Emily turned her head, she could see a distant flickering of lights that looked like fallen stars, slowly coming into view. "No one is truly no one. We all have a story to be told. Even if your story starts on a tiny harbor town others would likely call nowhere."

DARDURIN, A TOWN OF PIRATES

Emily

"Flynn! Aren't you a sight for these old eyes!"

The elderly innkeeper smiled as she pulled Flynn in for a tight embrace. Her cheeks were full and rosy, and her grey hair was pulled back into a haphazard bun.

After they docked the ship, Flynn took them directly to an inn. The inn was picturesque and clearly well taken care of. Children ran around outside chasing one another with sticks in a mockery of a sword fight, clearly used to the darkness as none of them even so much as stumbled during their game. A few of the children had stopped playing when they saw Flynn walking off the deck and into the muddied streets. They raced to him and managed to tackle him to the ground screaming demands of being let on his ship.

Levi barely lasted two seconds once they reached land before he made a point of informing Flynn of his plans to find beautiful women in need of company at the tavern. Lucas, on the other hand, left to find food and a quiet place to read. The two were polar opposites, or rather the three of them were opposites. Yet they all seemed to share the same goals which bound them together.

The woman hugging Flynn pulled away and turned her warm attention to Emily.

"Well now, aren't you beautiful," the woman began as she reached for Emily's hands, holding them in her own. "What is your name, dear?"

She looked briefly at Flynn who was already staring daggers at her with his stone-cold expression, then back at the woman. "Emily Underwood, Ma'am," she said as she bowed her head.

The woman's smile made her full cheeks look even rounder.

"Well, I do not know how you managed to get tangled up with this trouble maker here. I am Martha, but you can call me Mum. But between us, you are far too beautiful for our Flynn. He better take good care of you."

Emily's eyes widened as Flynn reached for their intertwined hands and pulled them apart.

"Mother? You are Flynn's mother?" she asked.

The woman laughed as Flynn pushed himself between them.

"*Emily* is not my partner, Mother. We simply met by happenstance and she will be on her way home by morning. We will need two rooms."

Martha's laughter slowly died down as she wiped her eyes and turned back to walk behind the desk.

"Then you two have come at the wrong time," she said as she flipped through pages of scribbled down names in an open book atop her desk.

"How so?" he asked.

Martha shrugged her shoulders and seemed to look apologetic, but Emily could have sworn Martha had winked at her. "Well, we are booked up tonight, unfortunately. Best I can offer you is one room."

"I am your son and you cannot spare two rooms?"

"And I am your mother and this is my business. You will take the one room and you will say thank you. Unless of course you would like to sleep in Mr. Balks staffing quarters again? I heard he is in need of a new barkeep," Martha said as she held out the key which gingerly hung on one finger, her other hand resting on her hip.

Flynn rolled his eyes and through gritted teeth said, "Thank you, Mother. Your kindness knows no bounds."

He took the key and began to make his way to the back of the inn, through the darkened hallways.

Emily stifled a small laugh with her hand. It all seemed incredibly normal; if she closed her eyes, she would have been able to imagine that she was back at home. She whispered a quick thank you and gave another bow of her head to Martha who only responded with a warm smile.

Turning on her heels, she followed after Flynn. If he grew up with Martha as his mother, it was a wonder how he turned out the way he did.

The book had never mentioned Flynn's mother or that he grew up on a small harbor town. It didn't mention his closeness with children or whatever had taken place with Mr. Balks that had caused him to sleep in the staffing quarters. The book had omitted all of it, leaving Emily feeling like she was staring at an incomplete puzzle. She yearned to ask him to reveal everything she did not yet understand and to clarify once more the things she already knew. Like how he came to be feared and known by all, why he held his compass so close to his heart, and even how he gains his victory in defeating the king. She wanted to hear it all.

He was rude and tasteless in his attitude towards her,

yes, but he wasn't the kind to harm anyone innocent. Or at least she didn't think that he was.

When they reached the end of the hallway, Flynn slid the key into the lock and unlocked it with a loud thunk. He opened the door and walked in first. He didn't even attempt to hold the door open for her. The room was dimly lit, but from what Emily could see it was in pristine condition. A large bed sat in the middle of the room. Above it, was a window that had a direct view of the ocean.

Emily started for the bed at the same time that Flynn threw himself down onto it. She stopped in her tracks as she watched him sprawl himself out, putting his arms behind his head as he gave her a smug look.

"What?" he asked.

"There is only one bed."

"So there is."

"So...you should be a gentleman and sleep on the floor," she argued as she gestured to the wooden floor boards.

Flynn smirked as he adjusted his shoulders as if he was making himself even more comfortable. "Yeah, that's not happening, Princess. But by all means, if you are incapable of sharing a bed with a pirate, then you are free to take the floor. I heard it's good for the back."

Emily scoffed as she put her hands on her hips. "You can't be serious. I am a lady, you cannot ask me to share a bed with—"

"You're not my type. So if you are worried about that, then you have nothing to fear. I have standards too, Princess."

Emily ripped the only pillow out from under his head and threw it back at his face as hard as she could. "I would bite my own tongue off before I ever looked at you as a romantic partner," she said, angrily pulling back the sheets and getting into bed. "This is fine," she grumbled, "come morning I will be back at home and you will be a distant nightmare."

Flynn gave a low chuckle as he shifted in bed. She looked over her shoulder to tell him to stay on his side but was met with his back.

"I only wish to see your departure, *Emily*."

Despite his foul personality, she couldn't smother the whisper of happiness she felt at meeting her favorite character, even if it were just a dream. Yet, even as she repeated to herself that this was simply a wild dream, a seed of anxiety slowly took root, convincing her otherwise.

She allowed the weight of her eyelids to close her eyes, slowly letting her tired body sink into the mattress. The events of the day had taken a toll, and sleep was quick to claim her.

BEING A GENTLEMAN

Flynn

A heavy sigh woke Flynn from his sleep. But that had been an hour ago, and he had remained awake in bed listening to the soft sounds of Emily breathing, since. Every so often, an audible sigh would escape her parted lips. She apparently had a habit of tossing and turning in bed and now, she faced him. It was his first time actually seeing her face and being able to take in the details undisturbed since meeting. The sun had only just begun to break past the horizon, shining into their window and highlighting her pale skin. In the morning light, he could see the brown freckles that danced across her nose and her rosy cheeks. Her scent filled the air. She smelled like Dardurin during the summers when the bakers would make their apple pies. She smelled like cinnamon and honey. She smelled like home.

Emily...so that is your name...

It suited her, he decided. At some point during the night,

a strand of hair had fallen down, partially blocking the view of her face. Carefully, he reached forward and brushed it gently behind her ear. He ran his thumb down the side of her cheeks and under her chin. Her skin was as soft as silk. Unblemished from any scars or shows of hardship and untouched by the sun. Something deep within himself knew that he wanted to keep it that way.

Truth be told, he wasn't sure if sending her home was the right choice. Not only for the fact that she might run to the guards, but what if something happened to her? What if she were kidnapped...again? But by a man with truly ill intentions. What if she went back to Oakden only to discover that everyone is already gone? Lucas' words rang through his mind. Why was she unguarded outside the square? Was she running from something or someone? There were too many chances and possibilities that ended in Emily not returning home safe. And if anything did happen, that would be on him.

You're not my type...I barely managed to say that with a straight face. She has the kind of beauty any man would be attracted to. She really is a siren.

Slowly, he ran his hand down past her neck and over her small shoulders. He let his fingers trail down her arm that rested beside her face. More freckles poured down to the tips of her fingers. It was his first time seeing them up close. Seas be damned. She was beautiful. He held his breath, not willing to let anything disturb her sleep.

When his fingers met hers, he noted how small they were in comparison to his.

She embodied a gentleness that did not exist in his world. Out at sea, it was one danger after another. She was a daisy in a bush of roses. If he sent her home, who knows what hardships she may be forced to endure alone. But if she were to stay, she would be guaranteed hardships. He did not lead a simple life, nor was he willing to walk a new path and abandon his revenge that was so close. It is not only his life that he must take into account, but the lives of everyone on the island. Levi and Lucas included.

The longer he kept her, the more at risk he put their carefully laid plans. Both of his friends had been through so much at the hands of the king. He could not allow himself to do anything that would distract him.

But his own resolve did nothing to quell his growing curiosity of his captive.

Where did she come from? Why was she here, especially now of all times? She seemed so delicate and so lost. Just as lost as he once was.

Emily stirred momentarily in her sleep.

Flynn froze.

After a second, she settled again with a sigh. Flynn's own heart beat hard against his ribs. Once again, the feeling of guilt took root in his chest.

She is a lady. She is a sleeping lady that trusts me enough to leave herself unguarded around me.

He made a mental note to talk to her about how careless she was. How could she just blindly trust him? He has given her no reason to. And his mother, he would have to talk to her as well. He knew more than anyone there was always an abundance of vacant rooms.

Flynn carefully pulled away from her, sitting up in bed.

This won't work.

He put the only pillow next to her so that he didn't have to look at her caramel freckles that looked like the constellations he would often use to guide himself home.

He couldn't allow himself to get distracted. No matter

how tempting that distraction was. He still knew nothing about her, or where she came from.

She said she was from nowhere. A girl from nowhere.

Flynn fell back and rolled over with a huff, using his arm as a pillow.

She could be anyone, and she is not worth risking his mission over. He needed to remember that.

It only took one more sigh through her parted lips for Flynn to lift himself from bed to lay on the floor. He could feel his self-control fraying like a strained rope.

I do not deserve a bed. Beds are for gentlemen.

He used his arm as a pillow again as he tried to let the sounds of crashing waves just beyond the inn lull him into a sleep.

Come morning, I will send her home. Or she will leave. Either way, all will be right with my world soon enough. No more doe-eyed sirens.

FLYNN WOKE early with the morning sun streaming into the room, even if just barely. The birds had only just begun to stir when he silently gathered his boots and his sword that had been scattered across the room, careful not to wake his sleeping captive.

Guilt was slowly becoming his shadow, following everything he did. He knew she must have been exhausted, so the thought of waking her so early did not sit right with him.

He left the room, turning the handle as he silently closed the door with a soft click.

He waited by the door for a few breaths just in case she began to stir. When he was only met with silence, he slowly turned and left down the hall.

As he walked by his mother's desk, he tried to keep his steps quiet. She was focused on the ledger and usually was unaware of anything else around her when she had her reading glasses on.

"You're up early," his mother said in her chipper tone. She looked up towards him, letting her glasses sit low on her nose.

"And you're meddling," he said back. This time, less worried about being quiet, he continued past her desk.

"Well, one day I will be dead and you will miss all my meddling."

Flynn sighed as he stopped in his tracks, and turned back to face her.

"Must you always use guilt?" he asked through an exasperated breath.

"Oh well, it does the trick, doesn't it?" She walked up to him and lightly tapped his cheek. "How is she?"

"Emily is fine. Still sleeping," Flynn dug into his pocket and pulled out three gold coins and placed them on her desk. "When she wakes, please give those to her as well as directions to the other docks. There should be a ship leaving in the coming hours. Tell her to say that it is under my order that they take her back safely."

His mother stared down at the coins across from her before bringing her knowing gaze back to her son. "Is that what both of you want?"

"Mother," he warned.

She raised her hands in a surrendering motion. "All right. I am just looking out for you, dear. She looks like a spitfire, she would fit right in here with us, if you ask me."

He leaned down and kissed his mother on her forehead.

"And I appreciate that. But please," he said pointing at

the coins stacked on the desk, "give her those when she wakes and send her back to her home. I mean it."

"Yes, yes. As soon as she wakes, I'll send her packing."

Flynn sighed and turned away from his mother. He left the warmth of the inn to be met with the brisk morning air.

This is the right choice. She will go home, and I will just be a distant nightmare. The pirate scum that stole her for a night.

But somehow, even he knew that he was lying to himself.

Flynn walked down the stone path until he was able to find his way to an open field where the horses were kept. Hopping the fence and made his way through the tall grass, some of the horses ran up to Flynn and he gave them each firm pats on their sides before pushing them away.

Flynn approached a large tree that was in the center of the field and as expected, Lucas sat below it making notes in his journal.

At the sound of Flynn's boots on the fresh grass, Lucas looked up and met Flynn's eyes. Lucas offered a slight nod and that was all the encouragement he needed to sit beside his friend.

"What are you reading?" Flynn asked as he sat down and leaned against the tree.

Anytime Lucas was alone, he indulged in the written word. Either by writing or reading.

"A poem. I am trying to find the meaning in it."

"Read it to me."

"What? The great pirate, Flynn Sawyer, knows poetry?"

Flynn narrowed his eyes at Lucas.

Lucas laughed gently. "Alright, alright. You just don't look the type, that's all."

"And the killer for hire does?"

Lucas shrugged his shoulders. "Fair point. Very well. It

says, 'If I kissed a fire, I know that it would burn me. Yet I keep kissing you in hopes that one day it won't hurt. The burns I receive in this love, are worth the moments of warmth that come before.' I have read it twice, and I have a hard time understanding why one would want to be so close to someone, knowing it will only hurt them."

Flynn found his eyes drawn back to the path that would lead him to the inn, back to where Emily remained sleeping. Back to that brief moment of peace.

"My father once told me," Flynn began, "that when he met my mother, it was like he had met a punishment perfectly crafted for him by god. They would argue over the smallest things. She would always win and he would let her. It made him happy to see how she would act when she was frustrated, knowing that he was the only one that could do it. He said that he felt it in his heart, this strange pull, the same kind he would feel when he was out at sea and missing home. He called this a siren's call."

"What does this have to do with my poem?"

Flynn chuckled. "Point is, you do not always choose who you love. Often times this choice is made without your control. And if the person whose song calls to you is a blazing fire..." Flynn trailed off, watching his friend. Lucas' eyes seemed to roam.

"Then you would kiss a fire." Lucas finished.

Flynn clapped him on the shoulder.

"Now, who has you reading these poems?"

Lucas' brown skin took on a pinkish hue. "No one! You know that I am only focused on the mission. I do not have time for such things."

"Ah, I see. Well, should you ever have time for something of this nature, enjoy it. We do not live easy lives. Who knows what day will be our last."

We can never forget this.

And Flynn promised himself he never would. He witnessed firsthand the toll his father's death took on his mother. He vowed not to subject any woman to the same fate.

CROSSING BLADES

Emily

"Father!" Emily yelled as she ran up to her father and jumped into his arms. He caught her, a slight grunt escaping him as he hoisted her up so that she was eye level with him.

"Are you leaving again?" Emily asked as she sat in her father's arms.

His brown eyes reflected her own sadness as his brows furrowed slightly. He brought her close to his chest and wrapped her in his warm embrace.

"There are still worlds to discover, my love," he whispered. His scratchy beard rubbed gently across her cheeks.

"Why do you have to go?"

He hesitated. "I promise I will tell you when you are older. You are only ten, you still have a lot of growing to do, Little Miss."

"Take me with you! I promise I can be a good sailor!" she yelled as her lips pulled back into a bright toothy smile.

"I bet one day you will be the very best sailor, and you will go *on every grand adventure that life has to offer you. And when that time comes, you take it, you hear me?"*

"Yes, Father," she said warmly.

"Tell you what," he said as he placed Emily on the ground. "Do you want to know a secret?"

Emily nodded quickly.

"All the adventure in the world can be found in a book. So, make sure to read, and when I'm back, you can tell me about all your adventures." Emily smiled, but it was not a happy smile. Her father put his umbrella in the stand and leaned down to kiss her forehead. "I will be back in eight months, my love. I promise."

Those were the last words her father would ever say to her. A year later his ship was discovered, wrecked on the side of a distant island. But not a single crew member was ever found.

What was found, however, was this very book. It had been in the Captain's Cabin packed neatly in a box with her name written on the top. When the royal navy brought this back to her, they refused to believe he was dead. But as the years passed, their hope dwindled.

I did tell you that this would not be a happy story. But I fear that it is too late for either of us to put the book down.

Emily's eyes slowly fluttered open to see plain brown walls...not green.

She slowly turned her head to look over her shoulder, but rather than seeing captain-of-nothing, all she saw was an empty bed. The only proof that he had been there in the first place were the wrinkled sheets and the pillow which had been pressed against her back as if he were trying to construct some sort of wall.

"That son of a..." Emily groaned. Is his ego really so inflated as to think she would throw herself at him?

She stood up from the bed and began pacing the room,

now that the sunlight had begun pouring in, she could see everything clearly. Everything from the walls and the tall wardrobe down to the sheets was a sandy brown. She walked up to the large window and leaned against the frame, looking out to the ocean. The clear blue of the water complimented the room. On the sand, Emily could see children playing pirates again with their sticks.

It reminded her of the children who would run around the streets of London in the early mornings.

Emily turned away from the window and left the room, closing the door with a soft click behind her. She walked down the halls, tracing her fingers on the wall and feeling each groove in the wood.

How come I haven't woken up yet?

She thought about this as she came to the end of the hall where she could see Martha hurrying about in front of the desk.

"Good morning," Emily said in a soft voice, careful not to startle Martha.

But the innkeeper jumped nonetheless and quickly turned around to see Emily.

"Oh dear, it's been so long since we have had guests. You are so pale I thought you must be a ghost," she said as she held her hand over her chest.

Emily brought her hand up to feel her own face, was she really that pale? Being in the library every day surely didn't help her complexion.

"It's alright, love, some time in the sun and some good food will have you looking fit as a fiddle in no time," she said.

Emily eyed Martha. "I thought you said all the rooms were full?"

"Oh," she began, "I did say that, didn't I? Oh well, must be my age," she said through a smile.

"I get the feeling that your memory is better than mine," Emily said softly as she passed Martha. It was hard not to chuckle at her meddling.

"Well, you can't blame a poor old mother for wanting to help her son with his partner now, can you?"

"Oh I'm not—"

"I have to say, it puts my heart at ease knowing he found someone. Call me old fashioned," she said as she looked down at the gold ring on her finger before looking back up at Emily. This time, there was more than cheer in her expression. Martha's eyes softened slightly and her shoulders dropped. Emily recognized that look as the same one she saw in the mirror most mornings. It was grief. "But, having a partner, someone to stand by you when the world seems dark, makes it a lot less scary. Heavens, I am getting old!" she said with a small chuckle. "Is it too much to ask that he find a wife and—"

"Have children of his own and a happy life?" Emily finished, already knowing from experience the next words the older inn keeper would say.

Martha blinked and then sighed, her smile reappearing on her face. "Yes. And to think, he has found someone so beautiful and polite on top of it all. It makes my old heart sing. He's too much like his father, that one. Always running off to his next adventure, keeping secrets. But secrets always find a way of coming to the surface. Just like the past, he cannot run from it forever."

Emily's mouth opened as if to say something, but what could she say? She was an impostor, she didn't belong here, and she tried to remind herself that this wasn't real. But the more time she spent in this world, the less it felt like a dream.

"I understand all too well," Emily said.

"Oh that reminds me!" Martha said as she shrugged her shoulders as if she were shaking away the sadness. "Would you be a dear and tell the children that they need to have breakfast? Food will be ready in the hall shortly. They should all be gallivanting around the beach."

Emily nodded. "Yes, of course."

She gave one last nod of her head to Martha as she turned and left. The slight breeze kissed her skin and the sudden chill soon melted away to warmth.

In the daylight she could see everything. The town was busy with people and everyone seemed to smile and make small talk with one another. No one seemed like they were in a rush. The houses were both old in their looks yet brand new, made of wood and stone with thatched roofs made from dried grass.

Emily stepped off the stone path and onto the sandy beach where, through the trees, she could see the children still playing pirate. She came to a stop under the shade of a tall tree and leaned against it for a moment, just observing them.

They all seemed so carefree, and above all else, happy and cared for.

The children began to scream, startling Emily out of her thought. But before she could react to whatever the danger might be, she saw Flynn chasing after the children with his own stick which looked more like a branch that he had chopped off a tree.

"Run!" one of the children with messy blond hair yelled through a smile that had been missing one front tooth. "It's the cross-bone pirate Flynn!"

"Aye!" Flynn shouted back in an over-the-top pirate voice as he came to a stop, pointing his 'sword' at the group of children. "It is I, but are any of ye man enough to fight the world's greatest pirate?"

A few of the children ran in circles, avoiding Flynn, but none of them tried attacking him head-on.

Emily stepped out from the shadows and approached the group. "Bit of an ego, don't you think?"

Flynn turned to look at her and his eyes shot open momentarily, as if he were surprised that she was still here, before they darkened as his lips curved into a smirk.

"It isn't ego Miss, if I am speaking facts."

"Then you should have no quandaries fighting me?"

"Aye, but what man would cross blades with a dainty woman?"

Emily scoffed as she yanked one of the ribbons off her dress and quickly fastened it around her hair.

"Can one of you, darlings, please fetch me a 'sword?'" she asked the children who had stopped their running and began to watch with wide eyes.

"Here you go, Princess!" one of the boys with red hair said as he ran up to her. "You can use mine!"

Emily took the sword and walked a few steps back from Flynn. She kicked her shoes off to the side and planted her feet in the sand.

"Fine," Flynn began, "I guess you are in need of being taught a lesson on what it means to cross paths with a pirate, Princess."

He stepped forward and brought his stick down in one swift motion, which Emily easily knocked away with an upward motion of her own as she stepped backwards, keeping her form straight.

His eyes narrowed at her as he, again, stepped to the

side. Emily mirrored his movements keeping the space open between them.

This time, Emily stepped forward, forcing Flynn back as their sticks clashed together.

Emily could hear the boys cheer and clap with excitement.

"Well, maybe my original assumption was right, may you be a thief? I do not know many princesses who know their way around a blade. I must say, you are better than I thought you'd be."

"I would say the same, but your footwork is sloppy," Emily said as she sidestepped and brought her stick forward.

Their sticks began to clash together in wide movements, each step Flynn took, Emily mirrored. It was as if they were doing a waltz of blades.

The next time Flynn stepped forward and their sticks met, he reached out and grabbed her wrist, forcing her still as he leaned in with only their 'swords' separating them.

"Thief, then? Who was your father?" he asked as his eyes narrowed.

"Wrong. I have been fencing since I could hold a blade. People think I only know books, but my father insisted I learn," she responded.

Flynn nodded his head, but before she could react, he pulled her stick forward and kicked her back so she was now unarmed. He walked towards her, tossing her stick behind him.

Emily shot up as one of the boys yelled for her to catch. She caught the stick just in time to block Flynn's next attack.

Their bodies moved in a dance known only to them. By now, more townspeople had stopped to watch their duel. Suddenly, Flynn tossed the stick into his other hand and ran it forward, swiping the rough edges across her cheek as he planted the wood against her shoulder.

Both of them were breathing heavily and Emily sighed as she dropped her 'sword' to the sand.

"Have you had enough, Princess?"

"You cheated."

"Pirate."

Flynn dropped the stick to the ground, but neither of them walked away. Her eyes darted between his and she could not deny that this had been thrilling. A bell began to ring and slowly both the children and the townspeople left, murmurs of being hungry spreading through the crowd.

Flynn and Emily remained standing in the sand.

"I'm sorry," he whispered.

"What do you mean?" she asked, but as the words left her lips, she felt something wet on her cheek. She brought her hand up to wipe it away and when she held her hand in front of her, a faint tint of red was brushed across her fingertips.

"I'm bleeding..." she said. "I am hurt?"

"Yes, I apologize, even though you did start it."

Emily shook her head. "That shouldn't be possible..." Emily dropped down into the sand and stared at the blood on her hands.

Flynn quickly dropped down as well. He grabbed her face and forced her to look at him.

"Are you alright? What's wrong?"

"I-I don't know," she whispered.

One can't feel pain while dreaming. She wouldn't feel tired or out of breath from running while dreaming either. Yet, Emily felt everything. The coarse walls of the inn, the water from the sea on her fingers, the familiar burn in her lungs from fencing, she felt all of it.

The truth of her situation had been staring her in the face since she first locked eyes with Flynn Sawyer, the crossbone pirate thief from her book. She was not dreaming.

But if she could bleed, logic would tell her that she could also die. Her stomach dropped and the world seemed to spin. She could die here and no one would ever know what happened.

She sat there in the sand, staring at the very fictional pirate she fell in love with over the last few years. Could she tell him? If she did, would he think she was mad and send her away? How is her being in his world even possible?

Questions swarmed her mind, none of which she had the answer to. But two questions broke through all the others, how would she get home? And did she even want to go home when staying here promised untold and unwritten adventures?

Flynn's brows furrowed and his grip on her face tightened.

"Emily," he said. "Are you well? Honestly?"

Emily stared at him. He was actually showing concern for her, even if it were out of fear for what his mother might say if she found out he had cut her.

"I just had a sword fight with a pirate," she said. Despite the seriousness of her situation, she couldn't help but bark out a laugh. "I, Emily Underwood, just had a sword fight with a pirate!"

Flynn bowed his head and chuckled. "Yes," he said, looking back up at her. "And you lost. Quite embarrassingly, might I add."

NOT EVERY PIRATE IS BAD

Emily

Mary Wollstonecraft once said, "*The beginning is always today.*" For Emily Underwood, that quote was undoubtedly true. She couldn't go back and change the events that led her here. She also could not change the sorrowful fate that was yet to come.

Still, time is a fickle thing, isn't it? If I were to apply the butterfly effect to this very book, something as innocuous as a butterfly landing on the wrong flower in a moment of time of which it did not belong to, could have catastrophic effects by irreparably damaging the future. Or, if you will, the arrival of a woman into a story that was never meant for her, could have dire consequences.

But I digress. What good is a storyteller if they do not tell the story?

The food hall was full to the brim with townspeople. The building was divided in two. Either side had four large benches that ran down the line, which easily sat ten people each. At the back, Emily could see the children all sat at one table, laughing and stuffing their faces full of an assortment of foods.

Emily was seated at the table nearest to the door on the opposite end, and beside her was Flynn. Across from her was Martha, Lucas, and the barkeep that Martha had mentioned earlier, Mr. Balks. He was a short man with tan skin and black hair that was slowly fading to grey. His features were sunken and he seemed just as grumpy as Martha had described him to be on their way to the hall. Even still, everyone sat pleasantly and enjoyed their food and conversation.

Heavens knew where Levi was, but during their walk up to the hall, Flynn didn't try to hide his speculation that he was probably drunk in a horse stable or in some poor woman's bed.

"So who cooks all this food?" Emily asked as she took another bite of her eggs. The moment she stepped into the building, her stomach began to growl at the smell of cooked eggs and fresh fish that had been spinning over a fire. However, when they set down the hot loaf of bread onto the center of the table, she barely stopped herself from drooling.

"We all have a part in it," Martha said as she also indulged in her food. "I help in the kitchen with the other seniors, Mr. Balks catches the fish, and the young ones clean up afterwards. We are a small group," she said with a warm smile as she reached for the plate of bread and slid it over towards Emily. "We take care of our own."

"That's incredible," Emily responded as she tried to pull off a piece of warm bread, but the crust wouldn't tear. She tried pulling again, but all she managed to do was mangle the corner.

Flynn snatched the plate away from her and she began to protest with a grumble of her own, until he pulled out a knife and began to cut away at it.

"We know that our ways are unfamiliar," he began, "we do not expect you to understand the importance of taking care of those around you." He put two cloud like pieces on a plate and reached for the butter across from him.

"Flynn!" Martha hissed. "It does not matter that she is not from here. You brought her here and that is what matters."

But as Martha continued to lecture him, Flynn spread the butter out across each piece of warm bread. It melted as steam rose. Once he finished with the butter he slid the plate over to Emily, but refused to look at her.

The corners of Emily's lips tugged up as she gave him a shallow bow of her head.

"It does not matter, Mother. Emily will be leaving today. Like I said, our meeting was an unfortunate mishap that could not have been avoided."

Her throat went dry and the bread dragged slightly, causing her to cough when she heard what he had just said. Lucas stifled his laugh with a sip of coffee, avoiding looking at Flynn and Emily.

"Could not have been avoided?" she whispered to him after she cleared her throat.

Flynn leaned in to whisper back. "Yes, could not have been avoided. You were a damsel in distress, Princess."

"Yes, except you were the one causing the distress," she hissed, putting another piece of the buttered bread into her mouth.

Martha cleared her throat and they both turned to look at her.

"Look at you, love birds. Already whispering and

sharing secrets. Don't they look like a proper couple, Mr. Balks?"

Mr. Balks just grumbled a, "Yes," without looking up from his heaping plate of food. This time, Lucas laughed mid sip, spilling the coffee around himself on the table. Martha ignored him as she continued talking to Emily.

"Well, I for one think you should stay, love. We could use a fresh face around here. And that goes for you, too," she said as she glared at Flynn who tried to avoid direct eye contact. "You have been gone for months and suddenly, you show up out of the blue with a woman and announce that you will be leaving in the morning. Most sons would at least stay for a few days and make sure their poor old mother was in good health."

"Yes, Mother. But we both know that age has not laid a hand on you yet and you are not poor and helpless either—"

Before Emily could stop herself, she slapped Flynn across the back. Once her hand made contact with a loud smack, she ripped her arm back towards her chest. Flynn slowly turned his head to look at her, his eyes were wide and his mouth hung open slightly.

"You struck me?" he said, astonished that she would dare lay her hands on 'the world's greatest pirate.'

"Well..." Emily looked at Martha who seemed to barely be holding back a laugh. "Yes. Yes, I did. That is no way to talk to your mother. Especially after she gave you a room and cooked you a delicious meal. The least you could do is stay one more day."

Flynn still held her gaze, amazed at her brazenness. His eyebrows scrunched together as he held up a finger as if to start to lecture her, but before he could get the words out, Martha chimed in.

"It is settled then," Martha said, clapping her hands in front of her. "You will stay until morning!"

Finally, Mr. Balks spoke up, having just finished his plate.

"Good man. Your mother has not stopped yapping me ear off all morning about how happy she was that you were back. Besides, I need some help at the tavern tonight. We will be having a fire fest," he said with a greedy smile.

Emily had a feeling that Mr. Balks was more content with the free labor than he was Flynn visiting his home.

"What's the fire fest?" Emily asked. It was something else to add to the list of things that the book never mentioned.

She never knew that entire worlds existed within the pages of the books she had been reading. She tried to avoid thinking about being stuck here and instead, attempted to focus on the conversation, but the more Emily tried to ignore it, the more real it all became.

Flynn took a loud obnoxious sip out of his mug of what smelled like coffee, before setting it down with one hand. "It is when everyone decides to get together and get proper drunk and fall asleep on the beach."

"You used to be more fun when you was a boy," Mr. Balks grumbled. "I'll tell ye what it is. It is like the old woman said, we take care of our own. We are a small group, even smaller as of late with the new laws from the king and all. Says he is going to burn all pirates from the land and return the seas to god, he says."

"Oh here we go," Martha said, rolling her eyes as she propped her head on her hand.

"You see, we wasn't always pirates. But the king, with the help of his cockroach supporters, raised the tax and the price of food a few years back. And if ye couldn't afford the tax, the Emerald Guards would be at your house by morning to take you away for breaking the law. We was watching our children slowly starve to death, what choice did we have? So, we all stole some ships and came here. We made this island our home. We still go out to sea to raid the royal navy ships for things like food and cloth, coin ain't much good around here so we take what we need to get by. Many of us go out and many of us never come back. So we drink to celebrate the life we made because unless someone kills the king, one day, he will find this place and burn it to the ground. Ye see?"

Emily was leaning forward at that point, yearning to hear more about this world she thought she knew. "So that's why you have the fire? To burn things on your own terms?"

"HA!" Mr. Balks yelled as he stood up from the bench and jumped atop the table. "She gets it."

"Ships be damned, how long have you been practicing that speech, old man? Hoping to advertise the tavern this year?" Flynn said as he took one last sip of his coffee and stood up from the bench. He turned on his heels and headed for the door. Emily had a hard time taking her eyes off of him. There was an uncomfortable pit forming in her stomach, she knew why Flynn would not want to discuss the king, but knowing all of this without his knowledge somehow felt...wrong?

"It ain't a speech, boy!" Mr. Balks yelled as Flynn left the building. "Just put me in front of the king. I'll stick him right in his black heart!"

Martha hit Mr. Balk's leg and he grumbled something under his breath as he stepped down.

"That's enough out of you. We both know if you saw the king you'd tuck your tail between your legs like a scared puppy," Martha said as she turned her attention back to

Emily. She nodded her head in the direction that Flynn left. "He's usually sensitive around these topics. But it's not my story to tell."

HOW TO KILL A KING

Flynn

Flynn walked down the stable hall kicking each door open until he finally found the one that held his drunken friend. Picking up the pale of water he had been dragging along with him, he lifted it over his head and poured it over Levi.

Levi shot up, gasping like a fish that was just yanked out of water, looking around like a crazed lunatic until his angered gaze finally met Flynn.

"What the fuck?" he demanded, wiping away the water from his eyes with both hands.

"You looked like you needed a bath. Time to get up, we are meeting with Lucas on the ship. We need to plan our next move."

Levi let out a breath and fell back onto the soaked hay. "And this couldn't have waited until noon?"

"Oh sure," Flynn said, "I will just go on and tell the king to please wait before you host your party, me and my crew need more time to plan."

It only took a few more kicks to Levi's boot and a few muttered curses for his friend to finally get up off the ground.

Everyone was already leaving the hall where he had just endured breakfast. He scanned his eyes over the crowd of people leaving, but he did not see Emily. Perhaps she had left not long after him.

Either way, today was important. Word arrived from one of his scouts that the king has left Oakden, only with one less ship in his fleet than what he arrived with.

Flynn opened the door to the Captain's Cabin where Lucas was already leaning over the desk near the window. Atop the table was the map they had used to note down the king's expected path, both from their own estimates and the word of their many scouts scattered across the sea.

Lucas looked up and when he saw Levi, drenched in water with bits of hay sticking to him, he crinkled his nose in disgust.

"Any progress?" Flynn asked, coming to stand beside his less-wet friend.

He looked down at the map to see where Lucas had been adjusting the lines with advice from the recent scout.

"Little. He left on time, which is good, and according to the letter, seemed to pay little attention to his missing ship. What of the invitations?"

Flynn pulled the carefully sealed letters from his back pocket and threw them on the table. They were sealed with an emerald color wax, the king's stamp in the middle. A two headed serpent. "They sent two, so I will need a date, as to not rouse suspicion."

"Figured as much," Lucas muttered as he chewed on his bottom lip.

"What name are you going by, Cap?" Levi said as he threw himself back in a chair.

"Lord Isaac Bensworth. Fifth grandchild to the Duke of Oshwire. Not important enough for a follow up to be sent to the duke himself, but important enough to be granted an invitation nonetheless."

"I could have just stolen one," Levi said.

"Yes, but we need the invitations and the guest list to be identical. Your role will come later. The longer we can last without the guards sniffing us out, the better."

Both Levi and Lucas wanted this just as much as he did. They needed this to go off perfectly. The king would be at the event, as it was, after all, a celebration of him. And he would never miss an opportunity to talk about himself.

Though, as this was a by-invitation-only event, an invitation which held the royal seal no less, this would have to be as real as possible. The best lies are always rooted in truth.

"So, who will be your date then?" Levi asked.

"Oh I am sure Cap will find someone," Lucas said. "Just make sure it is someone who will not ask questions when you disappear."

"Well, it will be easy for him," Levi said. "For you on the other hand, this would be an impossible task."

"Oh and I am so sure every maiden here is lining up to go on a date with you," Lucas shot back.

"Levi," Flynn said, looking up from the map to his friend who was wholly focused on irritating Lucas. "Did you acquire what I told you to?"

Levi laughed. "As if you gave me a hard task. I only had to break into the finest designer's house in all of Oakden, and steal four of the best hand-crafted masks all before I returned to help Lucas in case things on his end got hairy."

"I was only scaring some horses and lighting some fires. If anyone should need help it would be you."

Flynn pinched the bridge of his nose. "And where are they?" he asked in an exasperated tone.

"They are in a crate below deck, safe and sound. Oh, and while we are on the topic of valuables, where is your princess?" Levi looked at him through the wet strands of his brown hair. Lucas also stopped whatever nip he was about to say to focus on Flynn.

"Safe, going home come morning."

This time, he would not ask his mother for help. Flynn would personally see to it that she was on the boat after the festival, and that was final. The last thing he needed was another person to worry about. Another person that could die because of his own failures.

"So we are on this again?" Lucas said. "You are really sending her away?"

"I mean, you do need a date," Levi began with raised eyebrows. "And she is pretty."

Flynn shot Levi a look, wanting to deny it, but this time he couldn't. But what they were suggesting was impossible. Her being safe in his bed—in the Captain's Cabin—was one thing. But to put her in the center of everything? Unthinkable.

"All we are saying, Cap, is that it has been a while since you have been able to relax," Lucas mumbled.

"I kidnapped her. I hardly believe that she wants me anywhere near her right now."

"You're right," Levi said, standing up to leave. "She probably loves being alone in a new place, surrounded by people she doesn't know."

Lucas walked up behind Levi and smacked him upside the head, flicking water everywhere.

"What he means to say, is that you know better than anyone the fear that she might be feeling. It would not be a bad idea to relax before setting sail tomorrow. You and her included."

Flynn dropped his shoulders and let out a breath.

"Where is she?"

TO THE END

Emily

Emily scrubbed the dishes in the wash basin, coating the wet cloth in extra lye as it melted away in the water. Martha protested at first, but Emily insisted. It was the least she could do after being fed such a generous amount of food.

Martha, in a small way, reminded Emily of her own mother. Always fussing about and worrying for her child. But thinking of Martha only brought her mind back to her mother. Back to her home.

Guilt crept its way inside of her as she dunked another dish under the warm water. Her mother was probably worried sick. She had likely alerted the authorities by now.

And what of Ms. Lewis?

Her mind swarmed with thoughts of back home as she put the soapy plate in the next basin to rinse off the suds. What if the Green Room were to be discovered by authorities? Would she be punished for allowing Emily inside without a lady's maid?

Even more concerning, if Emily did not marry or at the very least meet with Mr. Brimsby, then her mother could lose everything. There was no doubt in her mind that she needed to return, and soon. But how would she even begin to make her way home when she had no idea how she got here in the first place?

Emily's shoulders sagged. It may even be the case that if she was too late, there would be no home to return to. And what of her mother then? Her heart sank.

I have to go home. It is my duty.

If her mother lost the house, she could end up begging on the street. With no one to claim ownership, and no way to secure a new house, she will have lost everything.

A pair of arms reached out from beside her and grabbed the plate she had been scrubbing in the same place for some time. She looked up and it was Flynn.

He took the plate from her and placed it gently in the clear water for rinsing.

"If you keep cleaning the same spot, you'll scrub a hole through it."

She looked up at him as he rolled up his sleeves and moved to stand beside her. He reached across to the stack of dirty dishes, pulling a plate off the top, dunking it in the soapy water. "May I?" he asked, reaching for the wet cloth that she held in her soap covered hands.

"I-yes. Sorry," she said, handing him the cloth. When his fingers brushed hers, she quickly pulled away and leaned over the basin to grab another cloth, dunking it in the water and rubbing some more lye into it.

Why hadn't he just grabbed his own cloth?

Emily reached forward and grabbed a plate as well and followed suit.

His hands worked around the dish deftly and they stood like that, washing the dishes, in silence for a moment.

"What troubles you?" he eventually asked.

"Why do you care?"

"Well, I may be a pirate, but I am not a monster. I told you I would help get you home. I still intend on keeping my word. So, if that is what you are worried about, put those concerns out of your mind, Princess."

Emily stopped scrubbing as she turned to him. The tips of his folded sleeves were damp with water as his arms dipped further into the basin.

"I have told you I am not a princess."

He smirked under her gaze, but kept his eyes on the dishes as he reached for another plate. "Aye, you have. But you still seem like a princess to me. So the technicalities make no difference," he teased. He seemed to be in a better mood, but it did little to improve her rotten one.

"Fine, Pirate," she said as she turned back to the dishes and continued washing. "I will have you know, I do not doubt your intentions to send me away. I am just lost in thought, is all."

"And what are you thinking right now?" His voice was deep and smooth. Standing so close to him, she was able to get a better look at his muscular build. Contrary to her expectations of a pirate, he was clean-shaven and smelled of oak and saltwater. His hair was tied back in a bun, with a few longer strands falling at the sides of his face. She let her eyes roam down his form, he had to have been at least a foot and a half taller than her. Her head only came up to his chest. Flynn cleared his throat and Emily quickly dropped her gaze from him and refocused herself. "Perhaps I *don't* need to ask what you're thinking," he mused.

Emily splashed some of the water on him with more

force than she intended, drenching his white tunic so it was plastered to his broad chest. He stared down at her as she slowly backed up, swallowing nothing.

"Perhaps it was an accident," she whispered.

He took slow purposeful steps towards her, shaking his head. "Perhaps you should run, Princess."

His meaning was only lost on her for a second until his lips quirked up in a devilish smirk.

"Perhaps..." she said as she took one more step back. Glancing behind herself she could see the door to outside hung open. She slowly reached her hand into the basin. Flynn narrowed his eyes in a warning but it was too late. With as much strength as she could, she dug her hand deep into the water and dragged it up, hitting Flynn directly in the face this time.

Emily shrieked as she turned on her heels and bolted out the door. She didn't know why she had done it, she should have her guard up. But a part of her felt like she knew Flynn. As soon as her feet hit the sand Flynn bellowed from behind her. She gave another yell mixed with laughter as she ran from him.

Emily chanced a look over her shoulder. Her stomach dropped as she saw how close he was to her. She picked up her dress and began running faster. She kicked off her shoes as she ran and barely registered the hot sand against her skin.

She darted towards the water but as she edged closer, she could hear him coming up behind her. The next thing she knew, she was in the air as Flynn grabbed her hips and spun her around, lifting her over his shoulder.

Emily was laughing and hitting his back, half expecting him to put her down. But when he started walking away from the inn and towards the water, she wiggled and struggled in his grip.

"Mercy!" Emily screamed. "I beg for mercy!" She pushed on his shoulder trying to squirm free and suddenly felt a hand smack against her ass with a slight sting. Emily froze. "Did you just—"

"Princesses should take their punishments. Behave or I might have you walk the plank," he said in a raspy voice.

Emily could feel her face redden as a familiar heat built between her legs.

No no no…he's a pirate. No, more than that, he is a fictional man. I cannot react like this to a fictional man!

Flynn walked into the water and before she could protest any further, he dove forward plunging them both beneath the surface.

The water was ice cold on her skin, but after being in the hot sun it was refreshing. Flynn released his hold on her, allowing her to swim free of his reach. When the water was shallow enough, she crawled forward on her hands and knees until she reached the shore. She fell back on the sand and caught her breath, only leaving her legs in the water. Her dress clung to her body in a way that would have embarrassed her for the pure impropriety and form fitting mess of it, had she been in London. But here, she felt at ease. Her chest moved up and down with each heavy breath. Her corset felt heavy against her, weighing down her chest.

I don't even have any spare clothes.

She could hear Flynn coming out of the water, but he wasn't nearly as out of breath as she was. He fell back on the sand right next to her. The sun warmed their bodies once more.

Emily turned her head to look at Flynn, but he was already watching her.

The heat returned as they stared at one another. His eyes left hers only to find her lips.

"I thought I was supposed to be a princess," she said through heavy breaths. "How dare you throw me in the sea."

"Sometimes, even princesses need to be punished," he whispered back as he inched towards her, turning on his side.

His words sent a shiver down her spine. The thought of punishment under his hand excited her. Every warning in her head was going off, they only just met, how could she let herself fall for his charms?

His hand reached for her hip, hovering over her for a moment as if unsure how close he was willing to be to her.

"Cap!" Levi yelled from a distance.

Emily startled and sat up, quickly pushing herself to her feet. Flynn sighed as he stood up as well, moving to stand behind her. She was suddenly reminded that they did not have as much privacy as she thought as Levi ran up to them. His eyes landed on her and roamed down her body. She crossed her arms over her chest, but before she could feel the full embarrassment of the situation, Flynn pushed his wet tunic into her arms.

"Put it on," he said.

Emily nodded and slipped it on, keeping her eyes forward on the horizon. The wet fabric tried to stick to her arms as she pulled it down over top of herself. When Levi was close enough to talk, he looked as if he wanted to make a comment, but one look at Flynn had Levi shutting his mouth. His eyes darted between the two.

Emily turned her head to look at Flynn and it was as she thought. His wet body was completely shirtless. His torso looked as if were sculpted out of marble and his arms were tense. No wonder he did not struggle carrying her. Emily's face heated and she was sure her cheeks had gone completely red.

"Ah," Levi started, rubbing his hand over the back of his neck. "Mr. Balks said that you told him you would help him work the bar tonight. He said he needs help setting up."

Flynn grumbled, "For fuck's sake," under his breath as he left Emily's side and pushed past Levi.

He didn't offer any final words to her, nor did he look back as he left.

Was it all in my head? I thought he was going to kiss me...did I want him to kiss me?

She shook her head slightly and swallowed whatever lingering embarrassment remained, straightening her back as she looked at Levi.

"Well, it's good to see you warming up to Cap..." His words hung between them with growing awkwardness.

"Yes," she responded, straightening out Flynn's tunic so it didn't look like she was wearing a giant's clothes. "Well, he is..." She searched for the right words but she wasn't sure herself. He was kind, trying to comfort her while doing dishes. He was fun chasing her about to get her mind off things. He was dangerous in the way he was starting to make her feel, and he was cruel in the way he seemed to make her heart skip a beat. He was all of those things, but when she tried to pick one, she could only say, "Nice."

"*Nice*," Levi repeated with a soft laugh. "That's a new one."

Levi looked down at the sand and then past her, but he didn't let his eyes fall directly on her. She wasn't sure what look Flynn had given him, but it was enough of a warning for Levi to know to keep his wandering eyes at bay.

"Does Mr. Balks always put the younger men to work?" Emily asked, trying to slice through the thick silence.

Levi momentarily met her gaze before he found a tree to look at.

"Yes, well, I have only been here a handful of times so I can't say for sure. But whenever we do come around, he seems to always be too tired or sore to lift much of anything," he said, laughing as the last words left his mouth.

The two began walking back to the inn but Levi kept a respectable distance. Flynn had distracted her from the worst of her thoughts which eased her anxiousness. But she still needed to find a way home.

"Can I ask you something?" she said to Levi as they walked through the sand.

"Aye, Miss."

"If you were stuck in the middle of something...how would you get out?"

Levi seemed like a better option to ask than Flynn. When Flynn was around her, he always managed to drag her thoughts to other things. Other things just happened to be his strong body, or his dangerous words that had a way of casting a spell on her.

"How do you mean?" he asked. His brows scrunched together and his lips slightly pursed. He wasn't a bad looking man. Quite the opposite, she noted. But something about her pirate thief sent her heart fluttering.

My pirate? No. The pirate.

"Um, well," she said as she clasped her hands together in front of her. "Let's say that you were stuck in the center of a story. What would you do?"

He looked off for a moment before his eyes once again met hers. His lips quirked up in a boyish smile.

"I would woo the women that book has to offer."

Emily sighed.

How could I think he would be of any—

"But if I wanted to go home, I would finish the book. I mean, every story has a beginning so there would also be an end, right? I would go to the end."

The end...

She let the idea sink in. In the end of 'The Adventures of The Cross Bone Pirate Thief', Flynn and his band of men subdue the King by breaking in during a masquerade ball. His men act as masked servers while Flynn himself waited in the Kings office. Once the ball was over, the king drunkenly stumbles to his office where Flynn delivers his words of vengeance, putting on a final siege alongside Levi and Lucas. All three men masked as if they were both the brigand and besieged. Levi finds his long-lost sister, Flynn gets his revenge, and Lucas deals the final blow. The ending was marvelous. But after reading it a few times, she couldn't help but feel a sense of emptiness at the end. The men were greatly damaged by the king's acts of cruelty and the aftermath of their trauma went unanswered.

Either way, if I could make it to the end alive...I might be able to go home...

Emily stopped as they approached the inn and in the mix of her warring emotions, she was at the very least thankful to have some form of an answer. She turned to face Levi who was standing behind her still. She grabbed the collar of his shirt and pulled him down, planting a kiss on his cheek.

"Thank you," she said gently. "Even you have your insightful moments."

Levi stuttered trying to form the words as he brought his hand up to cup his cheek.

She turned back around and headed into the inn. As she walked inside, she heard Levi call out to her.

"Yes—I am glad I could help, but what did I help with?"

"Everything!" she yelled back, turning the corner to walk down the hall to her room.

But now that I have an answer, will I be able to go through with it?

JEALOUSY IS UNBECOMING

Flynn

"I should throw you off my ship," Flynn threatened as he stacked another barrel of ale on the growing tower. By tonight, each one of the barrels would be empty, and men would still be thirsty. They went back and forth from one end of the bar to the other stacking barrels. Flynn did all the lifting while Mr. Balks ordered him around.

If it wasn't as a favor to his mother, he wouldn't be breaking his back for an old man, who by his age, was well past his expiration date.

"I would like to see you try. I may not be as young as I used to be, but I still got a strong swing in me ready to go!" Mr. Balks yelled as he flexed his thin arms. "Why are you more of an arse than usual?"

"What do you mean?"

"Your face looks like you just sucked a lemon thinking it was a beautiful woman's bosom. All scrunched up and sour with disappointment."

To make his point, Mr. Balks furrowed his eyebrows and pursed his lips together.

"You should be thanking me for helping in the first place, I have more important things to do than play bar keep for another festival of drunks."

"Like what? Play knight in shining armor to woo a woman we both know is too perfect to be in your league?"

"I don't want to woo Emily—"

Mr. Balks' previously scrunched features relaxed into a sly smile. "I never said Emily. So, you do fancy her then?"

Flynn groaned as he stacked another barrel at the top, leaving only one spot empty to complete the pyramid.

"I do not fancy her. I am a pirate, and she is a lady. What kind of life would we make? I'll tell you what kind, the kind where I die by sword or strung up in the gallows, and she becomes a widow. And if I don't die, she would be forced to look over her shoulder and live in constant fear for her life."

"Would she be in constant fear for her safety, or would it be you that would be terrified for her safety?"

Flynn scoffed as he dusted his hands off and walked to the back of the bar. The shorter man kept up with him, only looking at Flynn when they reached the back. Mr. Balks leaned against the barrel, crossing his arms over his chest.

"And I thought you were supposed to be a man." Mr. Balks said. "Yet here you are hiding from anything new or scary like a child."

"I am *not* a child. I am doing the right thing by staying far, *far*, away from her. Taking her was a mistake to begin with."

Flynn tried to take the barrel, but Mr. Balks swatted his hand away.

"Ahh, yes. The right thing. And tell me, is staying lonely

until the day you die, leaving your mother to worry about you being alone, the *right* thing?"

"Emily is leaving tomorrow morning," he reiterated. "However I might feel about her is none of her concern or yours. She will get on the boat, and go back home to wherever she belongs."

"Let me ask you something."

Flynn pulled the barrel from behind Mr. Balks, causing the old man to stumble back before regaining his footing. "You have been asking me things since I arrived."

Ignoring his comment, Mr. Balks asked, "If she were to take another, would you be alright with this?"

Flynn made his way to the front of the bar. "We do not even know one another," he muttered.

Would I be alright with this? It is bound to happen. She will probably take a man who has some land of his own. Maybe someone of noble blood. Someone sophisticated. Maybe they would have children. She would make a good mother.

"Of course you don't know her!" Mr. Balks said as he caught up to him, wagging his finger in Flynn's face. "You have hardly given her a chance. I saw the eyes you made at her at breakfast. They did not match your cold words."

Flynn came to a halt and turned to look down at the shorter, much older, man beside him. "Did my mother put you up to this?"

Mr. Balks shrugged his shoulders and shook his head. "Who knows such things? But if she had, it would be nice to have a favor in my pocket for later."

"You will die soon, old man, there will be no later."

Just as he was lifting the barrel above his head, Levi walked into the bar and quickly made his way across the room until he could throw himself down on one of the chairs.

"Levi!" Mr. Balks exclaimed. "You come here too much. What about you, eh? When will you find a woman to keep for more than a night?"

Flynn's arms strained slightly under the weight of the barrel of ale as he lined it up with the rest of the tower.

This time, there was no witty remark out of his friend, or even a chuckle.

"Emily just kissed me," Levi said in an astonished tone, just above a whisper.

Flynn nearly dropped the barrel, only just regaining his balance enough to set it down on the floor with a loud thud.

"Emily kissed you?" he yelled.

"I thought you did not want to woo her?" Mr. Balks asked, peering at Flynn.

Flynn shot Mr. Balks a menacing look before he turned back to his sleazy friend, grabbing his shirt by the collar and yanking him halfway across the bar. "Did you touch her? Did you throw yourself at her?" he demanded through gritted teeth.

Levi pushed Flynn's hands away and then ran his own hands down his shirt as if he were brushing off dirt. "Calm down! What do you think I am?"

"A whore."

"An idiot."

Flynn and Mr. Balks said in unison.

"Ha," Levi laughed, running a hand through his hair. "Didn't think you would be so honest. Tell me how you really feel next time."

"Did you?" Flynn asked again.

"No, you oaf. *She* kissed *me*. On the cheek. As a thank you."

"Thank you? Thank you for what? I have done plenty and she has not said thank you. If she should be saying thank you to anybody it's me," Flynn said, touching his own chest.

Mr. Balks snickered to himself in the corner, cleaning a mug with a rag.

Levi shook his head. "You're the one who kidnapped her, thinking she was someone entirely different. I, on the other hand," he said, holding his hand over his heart in an endearing manner, "offered her life changing advice out of the goodness of my heart."

Flynn scoffed as he looked away for a moment, regaining his composure before turning back to his friend.

"And what advice was this? Please tell me so I may also thank you."

Levi tapped his finger on his chin. "I don't know exactly, but it was good advice," he said raising his arms in a carefree shrug.

Flynn bent down and grabbed the barrel, once again lifting it over his head. His muscles strained as he lined it up with the top of the tower, and pushed it atop the rest of the stack. Once it was steady, he dropped his arms and grabbed the rag from Mr. Balks, giving his hands a quick wipe.

"Stay away from her," he ordered, flinging the rag over his shoulder to rest before crossing his arms over his chest. "She is not here to flirt with or corrupt, or *woo*. Just because your mother never loved you enough to teach you manners, doesn't mean you can get away with how you normally act."

"You know what?" Levi said, leaning forward to rest his head in his hands as he placed his elbows on the bar. "I was wrong. How could she not fall for you? You have such a charming personality. Baffling. Truly."

Flynn sighed and grabbed a mug, pouring his friend some ale from one of the tapped barrels and sliding it over to him. "We have to remain focused on the mission. We cannot afford for anything to go wrong."

"And nothing will. You know I want for nothing more than to find my sister," Levi said, breaking to take a large sip out of the overflowing cup. "But that does not change the fact that you still require a date to the ball. No date equals suspicion, and suspicion equals the king getting away. Who knows when we will have another chance at this. Whatever adverse feelings you are having, quell them. 'Sides, who better to take as a date than someone who already seems accustomed to the ways of the wealthy?" Levi finished, raising his eyebrows as he looked at Flynn.

Flynn shook his head. "I am not putting her in danger. At least not any more than I already have."

"Well," Mr. Balks interjected, placing a newly polished mug down beneath the bar top. "I may not be an expert, but I gather that women like being asked when it comes to matters of their future. You won't get anywhere by bossing her around all day."

"And," Levi said. "I heard the children around town screaming about how Emily defeated you in a sword fight."

"*Almost* defeated me," Flynn corrected.

"You cheated," Levi said through a grin.

"I'm a pirate."

"Either way, it is not like she would be defenseless. It wouldn't hurt to ask. Worst she can say is no."

No, the worst she could say is yes. Then I would truly be nonredeemable.

DANCING WITH A PIRATE

Emily

The town was buzzing with excitement as Emily walked through the crowds of drunken sailors and townsfolk. Just past the inn, in the main square, a wooden boat had been constructed for the sole purpose of being set ablaze. It burned away piece by piece, small dots of ash rained down, but no one seemed to care.

Music sounded from all around them, a harmony of flutes, violins and drums pulsed through the air. Emily sat down just beyond the circle of bodies and flames, slowly swaying in time with the excited music.

Couples danced around the fire, spinning in circles and joining arms, pushing each other away only to pull them close again. It was more wild and passionate than anything she had been accustomed to.

How am I going to convince him to bring me with him?

She toyed with the sides of the dress that Martha had given her. It was lower cut than what she was used to, but other than that it fit like a glove. The maroon corset sat low on her chest and narrowed as it fell below her waist. The rest of the dress was crafted from black fabric and pooled onto the ground.

"To the end of the book," she mumbled.

Like that is an easy task.

How would she convince him? Would he even want the burden of taking her along? It wasn't as though she had much to offer. When it came to fencing, she was well above average. That much was true. But beyond that, she was no better than a babe out at sea.

"Can I offer more of my helpful advice to make this night worthwhile?" A sly voice said from behind her.

Emily looked over her shoulder and saw Levi was standing behind her holding a mug of ale, leaning against a tree.

"What advice would that be?" she said through a smile of her own. Much like the life on the island, she was growing more comfortable around Flynn's men.

He pursed his lips and looked away, then looked back down at her, his smile turning into a smirk.

"The best way to have fun at a festival is through a wager."

"Oh and I am guessing you know this through thorough research?"

He nodded his head and plopped himself down next to her, keeping his drink steady. The smell of ale and quality cigars wafted off of him. There was something comforting in the aroma.

"So," she began, "what is your wager?"

He reached into his pocket with his free hand and pulled out a gold coin, holding it in his open hand. "If I flip this coin and it shows heads, you must drink this ale and dance with me."

"And if it shows tails?"

"Then I will do your bidding for the rest of the night."

Emily stared down at the coin before bringing her gaze back up to meet his.

"Right then, I'll take that wager."

Levi smiled again and handed her the mug of ale so he could free his hands to flip the coin. The fruity smell of the beverage permeated the air around her.

He balanced the coin atop his clenched fist so that his thumb was under the coin. With one flick of his thumb, it shot up rapidly in the air. Emily held her breath as she watched the coin fall into Levi's other hand. Once it landed, he covered the top of it so neither of them could see what side it landed on.

"You ready, Miss?"

"As I'll ever be, I suppose."

Her heartbeat picked up as she gripped the cold mug of ale, some of it had already poured down the sides and ran over her fingers.

Levi slowly opened his hand and in the flickering light of the fire, staring back at her was the head of the coin.

Fuck.

"Bottoms up then," he said.

She slowly brought the mug up to her lips, she opened her mouth and tipped it back, letting the bitter sweet taste of the ale fill her mouth. She kept chugging the drink until the final drops fell on her tongue, then cast the mug aside and turned her eyes back to Levi. She was never much for drinking in the real world. But in this world, the alcohol was more tolerable.

But even as she took Levi's hand, which was extended and waiting, she could tell the drinks here had a faster effect. The ale was already beginning to take a hold of her senses as Levi yanked her to her feet, walking backwards and pulling her into the ring of dancing couples that spun around the fire.

The music raced through her body as Levi pulled her close, spinning them in circles as they followed suit with the rest of the couples.

He linked his arm around hers and they danced in a circle before stopping and switching directions. Their bodies swayed in time with the beat of the drums and the growing crowd who begun clapping their hands in time with the quickening beat.

Emily threw her head back and laughed as Levi wrapped his hands around her waist and lifted her as she jumped, spinning them both in a circle before she landed on the ground and continued dancing in time with the people around them.

His elbow linked with hers once more as they spun over and over again, the fire begun to blur with the cheers and claps and beat of the music.

As they made another turn, Emily felt another arm link around her other side and pull her away from Levi, who also grabbed a new partner. She looked to her new captor and she was met with Lucas' beaming smile.

"Care if I cut in, Miss?"

She shook her head through her own laughter and grabbed both of his hands with hers.

He lifted their arms as they twirled around, lifting them above their heads which pulled them close and dropped them again which pushed their bodies apart.

As they danced, she was able to peer over Lucas' shoulder to see that Levi was now dancing with Flynn, who seemed to be cursing Levi out.

But a sudden rush of heat took over her body as Flynn's eyes searched the crowd, softening when they met hers.

The buzz in her head and the festival around them left her feeling euphoric as they spun around the heat of the fire.

The music picked up pace and they danced faster and faster, she let herself melt into the rhythm as a sensation of freedom raced through her.

Out of nowhere, Lucas dropped his hold on her sending her spinning off into the distance, only to crash into a hard body. Large hands quickly found her hips and guided her back into the ring. When she looked up, Flynn was already staring down at her. His eyes darkened as she threw her arms around him.

She let her nails graze the back of his neck as she pulled his head down.

"Here to kidnap me again, Pirate?" she whispered against his ear as he guided their bodies around the fire, still keeping in time with the music.

"No," he said, his voice was strained and his grip tightened on her hips, slowly moving lower. "I am here to rescue you. What kind of pirate would I be if I let somebody steal what is mine?"

Her heart skipped a beat as his words left his lips. *His.*

What would it be like to completely belong to a pirate?

"What if I wanted to dance with them?" she whispered just loud enough to be heard by only him.

His eyes roamed down her body with a look of possession that sent a shiver down her spine. "Then I would have to make it so that I am the only man capable of dancing."

They picked up pace and just as Levi had, Flynn lifted her until they spun around once, then twice, before setting her on the ground. Her arms once again finding their way behind his head as the music reached its peak, and ended with a final bang of the drums.

Out of the corner of her eye she could see partners pulling apart and she could hear everyone applauding both the dancers and the musicians.

Flynn and Emily had not yet moved. Neither one stepped away from the other. Their breaths rang out heavy and Emily found her eyes moving from his, down to his lips which were parted slightly. Instinctively, her tongue darted out to wet her own lips.

"So," she whispered, "who will rescue me from you?"

He shook his head slightly, still not pulling away. "No one," he whispered. "Who would dare steal from a pirate?"

His lips quirked up in a boyish grin, and for all she knew it was contagious, because the same smirk played on her own lips.

The music picked up again, but this time there was no rush in the beat. It was slow and easy.

Flynn bowed his head as he stepped back from her, and offered his hand.

"I am not sure I have another dance in me, Pirate."

He shook his head again. "How about a walk?"

She took his hand carefully, and when shivers ran down her spine at his touch, she told herself that it was the ale taking a strong effect on her body. It absolutely wasn't the dastardly pirate that only a few days ago, kidnapped her thinking she were some princess.

A PRINCESS, A PSYCHIC, A LIAR

Emily

"It's peaceful," Flynn said.

Emily looked up at him as they walked along the edge of the beach where the cold water met the sand. Each new wave washed away their footprints as they moved forward. Would the same thing happen to her when she eventually left his world? Would all traces of her disappear, like she had never existed? Or would parts of her remain?

New anxieties flowered in her chest.

This was never meant to be my life...it is not my story.

Still, even if it meant altering it, even slightly, she hoped someone would remember her. But to be remembered, one must first disappear.

"It is," she finally replied.

They walked hand in hand and the music and drunken cheers grew distant the further they wandered.

She looked over the dark waters, lit only by the crescent moon and the constellations which danced above her. How many times had she read this book, *his* book, and wished to be under the same open sky and near the same waters that promised endless adventure?

She still had a hard time believing that she was here, with him. His hands were warm on hers, and with each caress of his thumb, her heart threatened to leap out of her chest.

He just doesn't want me to fall, that is all.

"Tell me about your father, Henry, what was he like?"

As soon as the words left her lips, she wanted to swallow them again.

She hoped that he was drunk enough that he would miss her slip up. But then again, she was never all that lucky to begin with.

He halted in his movements, his gaze grew darker on her. This was now the second time that she had roused suspicion within him, and by the looks of it, he recognized it, too.

"How do you know my father?"

"I—" *shit.* How would she know of his father if they had only just met?

"And that night I found you, you knew about the horses, too."

"Well, I—"

"You seem to know so much of me and yet I know nothing of you. Why is that?" His voice hardened slightly.

Flynn dropped her hand, the sudden loss of his touch left her own hand feeling empty and cold.

Once again, the alcohol had clouded her judgment as she blurted out the first thing that came to mind. "I am a psychic."

He cocked his eyebrow at her admission and nodded his head as if playing along with her. "A psychic? Really?"

She nodded her head as she bit her lip. "Yes," she lied. "That is the truth."

I cannot tell you that I am actually a girl from London who fell into your world. That would cause a crisis within your mind by telling you that you yourself are in fact not real. That would go over just lovely.

Lying to him stung. However, she needed to get home. And so far, Levi's theory of going to the end was the only thing that made sense. Flynn was her one-way ticket home.

"Fine," he said, crossing his arms over his chest. "Then by all means, tell me who my father was. You should not need to ask if you truly possess these abilities."

"Right. Of course." What did she know? She tried to call upon her memory of each time she had sat down with his book. "Your father was kind. He loved your mother with everything in him. But he loved you even more. You even carry his compass in your pocket."

Flynn eyed her before he sighed. "You could have pieced that together. Tell me something only I would know."

Why do I feel like I am on trial?

"Well, your father..." *Think, think, think!* Emily's eyes met his, bringing up the past could either make him believe her, or it could push him away. She took a deep breath and squared her shoulders. "He is the one that taught you to sail," she began. "He tried to keep you away from the dangerous life he lived, but the ocean called to you. One of the last times you went sailing together was when he was captured by the Emerald Navy. You tried to fight them off, but you were still a boy. They tortured your father for no other reason than amusement and—"

Flynn held up his hand, silencing her words.

"Enough," he whispered.

His eyebrows pulled together as his jaw tightened. His

eyes searched hers as if to find the truth in her words, it sent a shiver down her spine that she couldn't be entirely certain was caused by fear alone.

Flynn let out a breath as his features relaxed. "Back on the ship," he began, "everyone told you their stories. I suppose you already know mine."

"Maybe, but that doesn't mean I won't listen."

Flynn looked out towards the sea. "I tried to save him, that day. But I couldn't. I stayed with him through the night. I kept asking, 'Why him?'. It was sunrise by the time I realized the answer to my question. There was no reason, they simply could. And I thought, 'What king would allow such cruelty?'. It was also that night that I realized what I had to do. I spent the next few months tracking down the guards who killed my father. One by one I sunk their ships and hung their bodies in the gallows with the fallen pirates. But I also left a message tied to each and every rope I used to hang them, 'Freedom for all, or freedom for none.' I left survivors on each ship, though. And after I managed to track down the men responsible for his death, years had passed, and my name was well known."

She cautiously reached forward and cupped his hand in hers. "I am so sorry for what happened to your father. He was a good man."

"Aye," he said softly. "He was. But good men often do not tell tales. I will never let the Emerald Guards enact such cruelty again. Soon enough I will put an end to all of this." Flynn looked down at her with a gentle smile. He was slowly, piece by piece telling her his story in his own words. "You know," he began, "you never told me your name when we first met. You told my mother, though."

Emily elbowed him in the arm. "You never asked for my name."

Flynn laughed as he held his arm. "Apologies, I was busy trying not to get caught and sent to the gallows."

She cleared her throat as she stepped away from him, extending her hand between them.

"I am Emily Underwood, daughter of Angus Underwood. A sailor *not* a king."

He looked down at her hand only for a moment before he once again took it in his. "I am Flynn Sawyer. A pirate who is a far better suiter than Robin Hood."

He bowed his head slightly as he lifted her hand and gently pressed his lips to the top of her knuckles.

"A suiter?" she asked, her heart once again pounding relentlessly against her chest.

His eyes met hers and he nodded slowly. "With your permission, of course."

"I thought you were to be rid of me?"

He pulled on her hand slightly, pulling her closer towards him. His free hand caressed the side of her face as his thumb brushed over her lips, which parted slightly at his touch.

His gaze only left hers to look down at her lips as he leaned in ever so carefully. When his eyes met hers once more, there was something uncertain in them. Like he knew he should send her away, just as much as she knew that she should remain focused on finding a way home. But both of them danced along the line between the ocean and the dry sand, not knowing if they would remain on solid ground or be swept away by the current.

"Would you like me to send you home, Emily the Psychic. Daughter of a sailor, *not* a king?"

She couldn't form words, but she felt her head shake side to side slightly, and that was all the permission he needed to slowly, ever so slowly, lean down and close the devastating space between them.

His lips were soft, and gentle upon hers at first. He dropped her hand and slowly gripped her hips, digging his fingers into her curves as he pulled her flush against him. She lifted her arms to fall behind his head and as she once again let her nails rake down his neck, his movements became desperate.

His tongue darted out and she parted her mouth for him.

She couldn't stop the breathy moan from leaving her lips even if she wanted to. Both of his hands were now on her legs moving lower and lower and before she could protest, his hands dug into her thighs and hoisted her up so that he was supporting the entirety of her body weight. He lowered himself to the sand so he was kneeling, his hands left her legs to grab her ass as he pulled her closer against him, fighting to annihilate whatever gap or space existed between them. He never broke the kiss, each second his touch grew more harsh, like a pirate fighting a war against time, fighting to get just one more taste.

Kissing him could be addictive. She felt protected, owned, and cherished by his hold on her all at once.

She wasn't sure if it was the alcohol, the festival, or the uncertainty of her future that pushed her to this point.

He ground his hips against hers, and an unfamiliar hardness pressed against her sex, causing her breath to hitch, and all of this to become all too real.

He slowly pulled away but only to press his forehead against hers.

Their heavy breaths blended together and Emily felt like she had just swallowed a jar of butterflies.

"Did you foresee that, Princess?" he asked, caressing his thumbs over her hips as he held her in place against him.

She rocked her head slightly against his. The waves in the distance that danced and blended with the darkness around them only deepened the tension between them, lulling her into a sense of romance and passion.

She needed his help, but it was not something that she could directly ask. She would need to use him, but what she was beginning to feel for him was too real, even if he was not. A new passion that she had never known was possible, was slowly flowering in her chest. And the most selfish part of her wanted to see it bloom. Leaving would mean letting it wilt away, yet what choice did she have?

"Can I ask something of you?" she finally asked.

She leaned away from him slightly so she could see his face for any disappointment or annoyance. But there was none. He smiled and nodded his head.

"Anything."

His gaze was possessive and loving on hers, and he watched her and waited for her to ask as if her wish would truly be his command. She swallowed her guilt as she leaned forward and wrapped her arms around him, pulling his head down so she could whisper in his ear.

"Take me with you."

UNDER HER SPELL

Flynn

I am a selfish man. No, I am worse than that, I am officially nonredeemable.

Flynn packed the last of his belongings that were scattered across the inn room, into his bag.

What am I thinking? She could get hurt. She could die. She could see me for who I am and leave me anyway.

And more than that, how had she known so much about him? She was a terrible liar. And out of all things she could have told him she went with psychic?

Flynn laughed softly.

He should be more concerned about her presence, concerned about her sudden appearance. Even if it was only a distant part of himself, he felt as though he knew her.

Last night when she asked to join him, he couldn't stop himself from saying yes. He was halfway drunk on both the ale and the feeling of her lips upon his. At this point, he was certain she was a siren more than a psychic, but he didn't care.

He wanted to capture her flowery and addictive scent into a bottle to keep with him always. He wanted to bathe in her smile and never see the light dim from her eyes. In a mere few days, he had grown more attached to her than what was safe.

There were so many risks of letting her come with him, so many dangers, but Flynn would die by sword before he let someone harm her. If someone so much as raised a hand to her he would cut it off and gift it to her. Show her that he could protect her.

And last night...last night they kissed.

She kissed *him*.

She kissed him with a desperation that mirrored his own.

In that moment, she could have asked for a star, and he would have found a way to capture the entire solar system for her.

"Are you ready?"

Flynn stopped his packing and turned to the opened door to see Emily. Her face was warm as always, and even held a glint of excitement.

He nodded his head and threw his bag over his shoulder, walking across the room until he stood in front of her.

"Are you sure this is what you want?"

"This is what I need," she answered.

What would I do if she said no? Would I let her go or would I take her anyway? Would I become every bit the pirate she thought me to be when we first met?

"Then we best not keep them waiting. Lucas is sure to be growing impatient and the longer we leave him unattended with Levi, the more likely it is we walk into a crime scene," Flynn said as he offered his hand for her to take.

Emily's eyes met his before accepting his hand. Her skin

was softer than any silk he had ever stolen before. Once again, his eyes trailed down her features until they settled on her soft, plump lips. Meeting her gaze once more, he noticed her cheeks were dusted pink. He leaned in ever so slightly, watching for any signs of hesitance or regret in her expression.

When her tongue darted out of her mouth to wet her lips, desire and need raged through him. His patience grew dangerously thin each time she was near him.

He looked away from her and cleared his throat. "After you," he said.

Emily smiled as she turned away from him, dropping his hand as she walked down the halls of the inn.

The second her hand left his, he wanted to reach out and grab her again. A possessiveness he never knew existed roared to life within him. With one kiss, she had undone him.

Flynn followed after her, only coming to stand beside her once they left the inn. They walked through the sand until they finally reached the docks where he had left his ship.

Seeing it again reminded him that he had no right to her heart.

I stole her. Kidnapped her and took her away from everything she knew.

And now, he was bringing her back to the ship only to steal her further and further away.

"Last chance to run, Princess. The sea is a dangerous place," he teased.

"Like I said, Pirate, I need an adventure."

He looked down at her as she walked in time with his strides. She was so small compared to him and his men. "It will be dangerous. Especially once we reach the king."

"I know," she said as she bumped into him on purpose. "But I also know that this is something I need to do."

"Why? Do you also have a vendetta against the king?"

Emily shook her head. "No, but I still want to help you."

A pang of guilt stabbed his heart at her admission.

She is too good. Too kind.

"Then," he said, looking forward to the base of the docks where his mother was waiting for them. "I will just have to do my best to keep you safe while you help me."

"I will hold you to that," she said as she smiled brightly at him.

The sun beat down on them, but it was not the cause of the warmth beginning to spread in his heart.

"Please do, Princess."

The area around the docks was full of the townspeople loading up everything from food and weapons, to rum to add to the water barrels to keep it from spoiling. It would be at least four days until they reached Butchers Harbor, and another five days from there until they reached the island where the king is holding his ball. They would need all the supplies they could get their hands on. Especially if his request would be granted.

Flynn tried to push down the feelings of unease that began to brew within him. Once they got to Butchers Harbor, the success of their plan would come down to one man. One very dangerous man, who only held loyalty to coin. He commands a fleet of thirty ships, and if they got him on their side, they could block off any chance of escape the king might have.

It aided Flynn, as he would not be moved by the king's title, but should this man be persuaded by another who offers more coin, it would all be over.

They came to a stop in front of his mother, who was

already pulling him into a warm embrace. He tried his best to quell his emotions.

He would do this. There was no other option but success.

He hugged her tightly before letting go. "I promise to return once I have done what needs to be done," he said.

His mother turned to Emily, opening her arms for an embrace. Emily smiled as she leaned forward to hug her. His mother squeezed Emily as she patted her back, and whispered something in her ear.

Whatever it was, made Emily smile. Which in turn made him smile.

She pulled away from Martha and nodded her head. Martha dropped Emily's hands, letting her walk past them to the ship.

Emily looked over her shoulder one last time at him, holding his gaze for a second before turning back and climbing the ramp to the upper deck.

Flynn's eyes followed her until she disappeared in the crowd of townspeople still loading the ship with crates and barrels of supplies.

When he could no longer see her, he let his gaze fall back to his mother who was watching him with teary eyes.

She cleared her throat and steadied her voice as she grabbed his hands in her own, holding them tight.

"Keep her safe and bring her with you when you come back to me."

"Mother—"

"No. I don't want to hear it. You're just like your father. Too stubborn to see what's right in front of you. Do you really think if she didn't want to be with you, she would be willing to sail across the seas to help you with something like this?" she asked, looking stern as ever.

"I will keep her safe," he promised. If the plan were to fail, he would at the very least be able to do this much. Above all else, he would protect her.

"Cap!" Lucas yelled from the helm. Flynn looked up and Lucas was waving one hand above his head, motioning for him to come. "It's time! We must catch the tide!"

Flynn nodded his head and turned back to his mother. She smiled and gave him one last tight hug before she released him. Flynn quickened his pace as he walked up to the deck and up the ramp, avoiding the townspeople that were leaving the ship.

Once everyone was off, Flynn kicked off the ramp allowing it to fall to the floor. He ran to lower the sails and secured them with a few quick tugs of the rope. Within a few minutes, the tide began to lower as the wind caught their sails, and they were off.

Lucas remained at the helm, taking the morning shift. Flynn would take the afternoon shift, and Levi would take over once the sun began to set.

With any luck, they could trade and barter for a larger ship once they reached Butchers Harbor. He had no doubt that they would gouge the prices and take most of his remaining coin. Their bartering etiquette was as nonexistent as their laws.

Once Dardurin was no longer in sight, or any land for that matter, Flynn allowed himself to go below deck where Emily was surely waiting.

As he opened the door to the Captain's Cabin, he watched Emily stare down at the maps that were still sprawled across his desk while she sat in his chair.

"We should reach our next harbor in a few days' time," he said, pulling her attention from the maps. He entered the room and closed the door behind him with a soft click.

Walking up to the desk, he pulled up a chair beside her and sat down, crossing his arms over his chest.

She smiled softly. "That is good, you are right on schedule then."

"Any prophecies you would like to share that could turn the tides?"

"If I tell you everything, it could change the sequence of events, could it not?"

"I thought you said having a psychic aboard would aid me?" he teased.

"Yes," she confirmed. "I did. And it will."

"But you can't tell me anything?"

Emily pursed her lips as she looked away, letting the silence grow before her eyes finally met his again.

"I will tell you when you need to know," she said.

"Then answer me this; Levi's sister, is she safe?"

"Yes," she whispered. "She misses him terribly, but she is alive and well. She is a fighter just like him."

Her words left no room for confusion or doubt. They carried a certainty with them that she was in fact alive. It breathed the smallest bit of hope back into him. Levi's efforts would not be for nothing.

Emily rose from her chair, pulling Flynn from his thoughts as she made her way to the bed. She pulled the covers back and began to slip beneath them.

Flynn tensed as he stood up and started for the door. She did not get privacy during the days back home, he should at the very least offer her this.

"Stay," she whispered.

Once again, desire burned through him, and his grip on the door handle tightened.

She would be his complete undoing.

He dropped the handle and turned back to face her. His

steps were slow and purposeful. The air seemed to thicken with tension with each step he took towards her.

His eyes roamed over her form like a wolf that hadn't feasted in weeks, and she was a doe, completely helpless.

Her lips parted slightly as her gaze fell from his, looking at her current state.

"Do you know what it means to invite a man into your bed?" he asked.

Emily still didn't look at him, but he refused to look away from her as he took the final step towards her.

He was falling for her siren call, but he didn't care anymore. He would let it consume him.

He reached down and gripped her chin between his thumb and forefinger, tilting her head up to face him. Pink dusted across her cheeks, and her eyes seemed to plead with him like she truly was his prey. His gaze dropped down to her freckles as he ran his thumb across her cheek.

She was his own constellation. She was his way home. She *was* home. Perhaps it was him that had fallen prey to her. Because whether she knew it or not, she was his to protect, but he belonged to her entirely.

"I asked you a question, Emily."

He said her name as a warning. That if she wanted to keep luring him in, above deck she would be his princess, but here, when they were behind closed doors, he would be her master.

She swallowed slightly and nodded her head.

"Do you still want me to stay?"

She closed her eyes, and like a gift, she nodded again.

His shaft grew painfully hard as it pressed against his pants, and his desire raged within him, threatening to boil over.

She was willing to obey him. It was a gift he would never

let another man know the pleasure of receiving. He leaned down slowly and pressed a kiss upon her lips. She moaned slightly, and it was all the permission he needed to trace her lip with his tongue and deepen their kiss. He moved to kneel on the side of the bed as he laid her back. His self-control teetered on the edge as another whimper escaped her lips. But the same desire that raged within him, commanding that he take her now, also had him pulling away from her. He inched back slightly so that their heavy breaths danced between them. Her clouded gaze held his as he towered over her, caging her beneath him.

Not yet. I still barely know who she is.

He gathered what little self-restraint he had left and dropped her chin, taking a step back.

"Get some rest, Princess," he said. He hated that he had to walk away from her when she was practically laid out like a meal just for him. But they both needed to rest, come sundown, he would need to have his wits for the long night ahead of them.

"The next time you invite me into your bed," he said as he held her gaze, "I will bend you over and fuck you until you know nothing but the pleasure my cock can bring you."

She closed her mouth as her eyes widened. Her face burned red and for the first time since he met her, she was at a loss for words.

The sight of her blushing face and nervous eyes was enough to make him want to rip her clothes off and take her right here. Everyone on the ship would hear her moaning, knowing it was because of him. He would make sure everyone knew who she belonged to.

But he would wait. Not forever, but for now.

He was already hers. She sealed his fate when she kissed him.

KING'S GAMBIT

Emily

The door closed, leaving Emily alone in the Captain's Cabin.

'I will bend you over and fuck you until you know nothing but the pleasure my cock can bring you.'

His words rang through her mind, only encouraging the heat that was building in her core. His darkened eyes watched her with an unwavering presence. In that moment, he commanded her attention. Just like at the beach, her body acted on its own, desperate to obey his every word, yet seeking his punishment.

She squeezed her thighs together, chasing the throbbing sensation that had taken over her body. She laid back in the bed and kept her eyes on the door as she carefully slid her dress up, exposing the wetness that began coating her bared sex.

She imagined Flynn spreading her legs, mocking her for being so desperate for him that she had become such a mess. Her fingers inched closer and closer to the source of her desire. They dipped into her sex and began to run light circles around her clit.

He would tell her to keep her legs spread or she would receive further punishment. He would bite down her legs, leaving marks for anyone to see, claiming her as his. And his tongue...

Oh god his tongue...

He would be mercilessly deft in his movements.

Her fingers quickened in pace, but she refused herself release. He wouldn't let her have release, not right away. He would play with her. He would show her that she was his to use.

Her breaths turned into pants, and she bit her lower lip in an attempt to stop the moans from escaping.

She reached down with her other hand and began to thrust her fingers inside of herself, while still keeping her other hand focused on her clit.

She imagined him staring down at her, with dark reproachful eyes as he leaned in close to whisper in her ears. She fantasized of the pain and ecstasy from the tip of his cock lining up with her entrance, before ruthlessly thrusting himself inside of her.

'Good girl, Princess.'

It was her own imagination, but even the thought of him praising her as he carried out her punishment was enough to send her over the edge. Her sex quivered around her fingers as her back arched. Rapture washed over her body, drowning her in wave after wave of pleasure.

She dropped her hands to her side and laid there, panting on the bed.

What am I doing?

She pulled the blankets over her, and rolled on her side.

This was just a moment of weakness. That is all. He. Is. Not.

Real.

She scolded herself as she closed her eyes tight. He wasn't real. Not really. And once they killed the king, she would be gone. She would be back home in London, she would marry Lord Brimsby, and she would save her mother's house.

I am a girl from nowhere. I do not get to sail off into the sunset.

"Your king will fall, and with it, your wretched empire of darkness," Levi growled, glaring at Emily.

"That is how you can tell he is losing," Lucas said from behind Emily.

She sat on the flat top of a barrel across from Levi, staring down at the makeshift table that held their chess board. The sun was setting, casting the ship and everything on it in a beautiful orange glow.

So far, she had managed to take four of Levi's pawns, both of his rooks, and one knight. She had opened with the King's Gambit and he had foolishly accepted, even teasing her that it was a sloppy opening. The King's Gambit was more of a romantic approach, but it was a double-edged sword. The key is to trick your opponent into thinking the king is vulnerable, moving its pawns away, leaving the king susceptible to an attack. Ruled by greed and a desire for victory, the opponent foolishly accepts, thinking the game will be over shortly. But, in the facade of victory, that is when the opponent will fall, piece by piece, until the game is over. That is the whole point of any gambit. You must first sacrifice something to gain something.

"I'm not losing," Levi snapped. His face was scrunched

as he leaned forward. His hands danced over his own players, hesitating before eventually moving another pawn two spaces forward. "I am concentrating. It doesn't matter how many players I lose, the game continues until the king falls."

"Or, you surrender," Emily teased. "Besides," she said, taking another one of his pawns with her knight. "You shouldn't be so ready to sacrifice your pawns. If you can get them to the other side of the board, you can get a key player back."

Levi answered her taking of his pawn by using his queen to knock her horse down. "And what are the odds of that, with only a few left standing? I say go right for the kill. Cut the king down by any means necessary."

"Well then," Emily moved her own queen forward, lining it up with both his queen and king, "will you sacrifice your queen to keep your king? Or will they fall together? Though, I am sorry to say but that's Checkmate."

Emily smiled as she sat back. With his queen taking the bait and leaving the king's side, it allowed her bishop to have full access to the king. Now, no matter where his king moved, it would fall.

"Well, I'll be damned," Lucas said, crossing his arms over his chest. "That *is* checkmate."

Levi sighed as he stood up. "Good game, Princess. You will have to teach me that opening the next time we play."

"Looks like you finally met your match," Lucas quipped. His lips quirked up in a grin as Levi rolled his eyes. The two of them were always fighting and at each other's throats, but beneath all of that, Emily could tell that they cared deeply for one another.

As Levi turned and made his way to the helm and Lucas disappeared below deck, Emily began picking up the pieces and putting them back in the little satchel they came out of.

It's not like she was avoiding Flynn, but being around him made her heart uneasy. She was already lying to him about who she was, and now she was also falling for someone that wasn't even real.

The cold wind blew in from the sea, making her body shiver slightly.

But it feels real.

She could feel the coldness of the wind, she could smell the salt from the sea, she could feel the roughness of his touch and the warmth of his breath when they danced in front of the fire. Were these things not real? Even if just temporary? Could they not be real in the moment?

"Coin for your thoughts?" A familiar voice said from behind.

She dropped the last pawn into the satchel and tied it off, leaving the bag on the makeshift table. Emily turned around to see Flynn leaning against the mast, staring down at her.

"My thoughts are worth more than a coin, Pirate."

"I don't disagree, Princess. However, it's a bit unfair, don't you think?"

"Unfair? How so?"

"Well," he said, leaving the mast and coming to stand in front of her, "you seem to know everything about me and yet I know almost nothing about you, other than you claim to be a girl from nowhere."

Emily took a step back and turned away from him so she could lean over the side of the ship. She looked out at the water that danced with different colors as Flynn came to stand beside her.

"My father was a sailor," she finally said.

"Not a pirate nor a king," he said softly.

She shook her head. "He was a trader. He would go out

and barter and sell goods, and return home with coin and stories to tell. He would always bring back gifts for my mother. They were in love. So in love that sometimes I had a hard time understanding how one person could love another *that* much."

"He sounds like a good man."

Emily looked at Flynn and offered a warm smile. "He was."

"Was?" Flynn questioned, turning his body to face her fully.

"He went out to sea ten years ago. He promised me he would return in eight months time and that was the last thing he ever said to me. His ship was found abandoned a few months later. They believed his ship capsized and most likely killed everyone on board. When they told this to my mother, she refused to believe it. Each night I would listen to her pray for my father's safe return. Despite her broken heart, eventually, she had to start making hard decisions. Just like me."

Flynn's eyes were sympathetic on hers. "What decisions?"

"Well, where I am from, women cannot own property."

"You aristocrats and your rules. Such pointless laws. And yet the wealthy call *us* barbaric. Such laws should never exist."

Emily laughed. "Yes, well, most people from my home would disagree with you. So, unless I marry a man, my mother will lose every last piece of my father that still exists within her home." Emily let the words hang between them. Flynn's eyes widened in realization as he leaned back against the wall of the ship. His eyebrows furrowed and his lips curled back in disgust.

"So you are being sold off? Like cattle?"

"It's not as bad as you make it sound, but yes. Once I return home, I am to wed a lord. I hardly know him, but he has enough money to save my mother's house."

"No."

Emily looked up at him, this time leaning back herself. "No? What do you mean no?"

"*No*," Flynn repeated. "No, you will not marry him. Have you even had a conversation with him? Do you know if he is kind, or decent, or fair?"

She scoffed. "And I am guessing you have the ordained authority to make such a command? And even if I do not know him, I am sure he is all of those things. He is a lord."

An empty laugh rolled over him. "And because he holds a royal title, he must be good then?"

Emily's brows furrowed in frustration. "You do not understand, Flynn," she said in a pleading tone—wanting, *needing,* him to understand. "This is my duty. I have no choice in this."

"And if you had a choice?" he asked, taking a step closer.

She held his gaze, releasing a breath before shaking her head. "I do not."

"But if you did, would you marry this man? Or would you give the honor to someone else?" He took one last step forward until her back was pressed against the wall of the ship. He reached forward and tucked a strand of hair behind her ear before lowering his touch to caress the underside of her chin. "Answer me, Emily," he said in a firm but pleading tone.

"Of course not. But—"

"Then it is settled. I will kidnap you again if I must. You will not marry someone you do not love. After we are done here, I will buy your father's house so you may keep it."

"Flynn..." She wanted to argue, and tell him that it

wasn't possible, but she did not want his warm touch or his possessive words to disappear.

"I mean it. It is the least I can do after all you have promised to do for me, my Fortune Teller. I would be wise to keep you by my side."

He still held her chin in his rough grip, his eyes danced between hers and her lips. Flynn leaned in slightly. Emily turned her head to look for where Levi was standing, but Flynn pulled her face to look back at himself.

"He cannot see us from there, the masts are in the way." Flynn pushed his leg in between hers and Emily felt wetness begin to form where she met his thigh. She opened her lips and let out a breathy moan as Flynn leaned down to whisper beside her ear, "do you want me to touch you, Emily?"

His rough voice sent shivers down her spine.

Her words came out breathlessly as she nodded her head. "Yes."

Flynn kissed a line down her neck, nipping, biting, and marking her as his. The pressure on her sex left as he lowered himself to the ground to be kneeling before her.

"Then do not make a sound, Princess. I do not want anyone else to hear your sweet cries. They are only for me, do you understand?" He pulled up her dress slowly, the fabric raking against her skin. Desperation grew within her as his heated gaze never left hers. "Nod if you understand, Princess."

His demand made her want to surrender herself to him. Emily nodded her head, pulling her bottom lip into her mouth with her teeth. Flynn lifted her leg to rest on his shoulder as he left bite marks on her inner thigh.

"Good girl," he whispered against her skin.

A SIREN'S CALL

Flynn

*S*_he will be my end._

His hands gripped her thigh hard enough to leave marks as he kissed his way up her leg, closer to what he wanted most. He wanted her taste on his tongue and her breathless moans in the air. He wanted to possess her, to bend her to his will. He wanted to be the only one to praise her and punish her.

Flynn bunched the dress at Emily's hips as her hands came down on his shoulders. He looked up at her and her eyebrows were pinched together as she bit her lower lip.

He moved to hold the fabric of her dress in one hand, using his other to grab one of her wrists. Everything about her was delicate and worthy of worship. He held her worried gaze as he turned her arm over so he could kiss the inside of her wrist and down to the center of her palm.

"Do you want this, Emily?" he whispered against her skin.

"Yes, but you do not have to—"

"Then let me take care of you." Flynn dropped her arm and moved back to placing tender kisses on her inner thigh. With each press of his lips on her velvet soft skin, he was gifted with a hitch of her breath or a soft whimper. "Your pleasure is what I want, Princess. And I am a man desperate to be rewarded."

He closed the space between them, pressing his mouth against her dripping sex. Warmth flooded his mouth as he ran his tongue between her folds. Emily's head fell back against the wall and her hands tightened on his shoulders. Ecstasy coated his tongue as he wrapped a hand around her, cupping her ass and pulling her harder against him so she was nearly off the ground. Emily gasped and her leg tensed on his shoulder.

It was as if his deepest cravings were finally being sated. He did not care if it would be seen as indecent, he wanted to ravish her. With the next deft swipe of his tongue, a low moan ripped from Emily's throat as her hips began to rock against his face, adding more pressure.

Flynn added a second hand to grab her ass as he lifted her higher, so her back was against the wall and she was completely riding his face. He kissed her deeper, harder, *faster*.

Flynn looked up and held her heated gaze. Her mouth hung open with desperate breaths as she looked down at him. Her face had gone completely red. Flynn pressed his tongue deeper and Emily's eyes closed as her thighs trapped his head.

"Flynn," she begged in a whisper. "Please. Oh god, please...don't stop."

He kept licking and stroking her with his tongue, his own hardness pressed against his pants to the point that it was almost painful. But tonight, he would not take from her. Tonight, he would only give.

Emily's legs shook and her head fell back as she dropped his shoulders and slapped her hands over her mouth, muffling a moan as she released on his tongue. Refusing to let a drop of her pleasure go to waste, Flynn swallowed all of her. Emily's sweetness and scent mixed with the breeze from the sea, and it was as if all his sins had been forgiven and he was at Heaven's Gates.

He kissed her sex one last time and her legs quivered against the sides of his head.

"Good girl," he praised as he kissed her thigh once more.

"So good," she breathed out.

Flynn carefully lowered her legs to the ground, keeping a firm hold on her waist so she wouldn't fall. He couldn't stop the smirk from playing at his lips as her legs wavered under herself.

"I should always wish to please you, Princess. And maybe—" he fixed her dress so that her legs were covered, "—punish you when I see fit."

This time, rather than some quip or some witty remark, Emily just smiled warmly at him as she leaned forward. She cupped his face in her soft hands and pressed her lips against his own. Her kiss was soft and tender, and full of care.

When she pulled away, he could feel his cheeks heating as if he hadn't just brought her entirely new pleasures.

"I would like that very much, Pirate." Her voice was seductive but he did not miss her own smirk, smugly resting on her face.

Flynn sighed and wrapped his arms around her waist

and pulled her flush against him until he could rest his head against her stomach.

"Ah, Princess. You really will be my undoing."

FLYNN TOOK another sip out of the bottle of rum as he looked over a sea of blackness. What he and Emily had done would stay burned in his mind for all his days. It was more than someone like him could hope for.

But...what can I offer her?

He had no home, only stolen coin, and he had no vision of his future beyond killing the Emerald King. What happens after?

"I thought only Levi tried to solve his problems at the bottom of a bottle," Lucas said as he came to stand next to Flynn. He leaned over the edge and swiped the half empty bottle from Flynn, taking a sip.

"Aye, most of the time that assumption would be correct," he mumbled.

"But it is not this time? What troubles you? Is it perhaps a certain princess stowaway?" he asked, taking another sip of rum. Flynn looked to his side and held his friend's gaze. He was still wearing that old black eye patch from when they first met.

"She vexes me. I know nothing about her, and I have nothing to offer someone like her. Yet here she is. What if I can't keep her safe?"

Lucas nodded his head. "You're very well right. You might not have much to offer, and she might get hurt—"

"Thank you, I feel much better."

"But, if you do not try to stand by her now, you will regret what might have been for the rest of your life."

"That's rich, coming from you." Flynn cocked a grin at Lucas as he took his bottle back to take another swig.

He stayed out of his crew members' personal affairs for the most part, not wanting to complicate things. Though, it was hard to ignore how Lucas looked whenever Levi disappeared to the brothels or took a new woman to his bed each night.

Lucas furrowed his brows and scowled. "I have no idea what you are talking about."

"Sure you don't."

"I don't!" Lucas snapped. He ran his hand through his hair and released a held breath as he looked over to where Levi was steering the ship. "He is a friend," Lucas confessed. "And he only likes women. There is no point in saying anything if it means losing him as a friend. Our times are not kind to men like me. I want to be by his side. Even, if that means watching him love someone else." Lucas spoke with a finality in his tone that told Flynn the conversation was over.

Flynn figured out not long after recruiting Lucas that he preferred the company of men. Not that it mattered though, as long as he could hold a sword Flynn cared not who Lucas sought pleasures with. It was all the same in the end. Where you come from, which God you sell yourself to, who you prefer to share a bed with, whether you were a man, woman, or anything else, none of it mattered. They were pirates not nobles. Still, he knew it must not have been easy for Lucas to have confided in him. No matter how close they were, it remained a risk nonetheless.

"Besides," Lucas continued, turning his attention and the conversation back to Flynn. His eyes looked fallen like he was already preparing himself for rejection for something he hadn't even said. "Emily cares for you. I don't know why, God knows it's not your personality, but she does. At least you have a chance if you don't royally fuck it up. And if it's any reassurance, you do not need to know everything about who someone is to care for them."

Lucas' lips curved up in a soft smile.

"Easier said than done."

How do I avoid fucking up when I am with a woman like her? I completely lose myself.

A GOOD TEACHER

Emily

Beginning a relationship can often feel daunting, like stepping into darkness where you can't tell if each step is on glass or stone.

The cool breeze of the salt kissed sea brushed against Emily's skin as she leaned against the wall of the ship, watching Flynn at the helm. Every so often he would look down at that golden compass before adjusting their course.

Last night, she had opened up about her father. But still, Flynn said nothing of his own. She knew enough from the book that it was not a pleasant memory. But she wanted Flynn to trust her enough to tell her himself.

But do I deserve his trust? Will I not abandon him when the time comes? What honesty have I offered him in all of this?

Her growing guilt was an entirely different beast she had to battle. Alongside her growing consciousness of Flynn. She was all too aware of his presence and the desire that flowered in her chest any time he poured his attention upon her.

All morning he had tried to act as if nothing had transpired between them the night before, but she could still catch glimpses of his knowing gaze when he thought no one was watching.

Each time their eyes met, she felt as though he was slowly pulling apart her resolve to go home, piece by piece. She was content to be here on his ship, sailing across the open ocean. She could pretend like nothing else mattered.

"You are like a pair of love sick puppies," Levi said as he unpacked a crate of food next to her. He lifted the lid to the crate and pulled out some cloth wrapped cheese and handed a bundle to her.

She held it in her hands and carefully unwrapped it to reveal two large pieces of cheese and a few grapes.

"Go," Levi said. "Bring him some food as well, and perhaps strike up a conversation. You're making me sick with all yer pining."

Emily looked at him and saw he was grinning ear to ear. She nodded her head and held the bundle of food carefully as she walked across the deck. Flynn quickly caught her gaze and he watched her as she approached. His hardened expression softened as she grew closer. It sent her already nervous heart galloping about in her chest.

"Come to relieve me of my duties, Princess?" Flynn teased. His dark eyes watched her every move as she took her final steps towards him. She once again unwrapped the food from the cloth, revealing the cheese and fruit.

"I have come to give you food so you don't starve to death."

Emily removed a handful of grapes from their stems, letting them roll around in her palms. She lifted her hand with the grapes to Flynn but he just stared at them.

"What?" she asked.

"I am steering the ship so that we may avoid certain death. Feed me."

Emily gave a sharp laugh. He was acting like a child. "Feed you?" she asked, her voice slightly higher in pitch.

"Yes," he confirmed with a slight nod of his head. His eyes practically glistened with amusement. "Feed. Me."

He opened his mouth to show his tongue and teeth, waiting to be fed the fruits. Emily could feel her cheeks heat with the memories of what that tongue was capable of. She huffed out an exasperated sigh and used her index finger and thumb to grab a grape from her palm while she held the cloth wrapped food in her other hand. She lifted the grape up to Flynn's mouth and carefully popped it in.

He bit down on the fruit as he closed his mouth. They repeated this process until the food was gone. Every so often he would stop to look back at that golden compass, only making her curiosity grow and fester.

"Is there a grand story behind it?" she finally asked, trying to give Flynn an opportunity to open up as he swallowed the last piece of cheese.

Flynn followed her gaze and looked down at the compass in his hand.

Running his thumb over the golden ridges, he smiled as he nodded his head. "It is like you said on the beach, he was a sailor, much like your father. He always spoke about wanting me to use his compass. I even had it on the day that he died. He wanted me to one day use it to make my own path and find my own adventure," Flynn said softly. He chuckled. "I don't know if usurping the king was exactly what he had in mind, but I will forge on and find a true adventure one day."

Emily reached for Flynn's arm and pet it as he spoke, trying to offer any comfort she could. He looked down at her with gentle eyes and a kind smile as he continued to talk about his father. She did not know when, but at some point, there had been a fundamental shift in their relationship. The loneliness that had harbored itself in her chest became less and less present with each day they spent together.

"I know this isn't what he would have wanted, but this is what all of our people, not just my own, need. The king's reign has destroyed almost everything. We cannot live on like this."

Emily squeezed Flynn's arm earning another look of adoration from him.

"Your father would be so proud," she whispered as she stood up on her toes and leaned forward, placing a soft kiss on his cheek.

Flynn looked back at the water. "You really are a siren, Princess," he whispered.

"And whose fault is that?" Emily asked.

He looked down at her again and almost looked shocked before he threw his head back with a laugh. "Well, I guess that is my fault as well then. This pirate apologizes for corrupting a woman of your standing, Princess."

Emily's own lips parted for a small laugh. "Good, at least you're finally learning some manners."

"Tell me more about your father, did you ever go out sailing with him?"

She shook her head. "I was still young when he died. He went out one day, and never came back. He always promised that one day he would teach me..." Her voice trailed off as she called upon her memories of their last day together. She could understand Flynn's need to act. Her father had been taken by the sea, not an evil king. And yet, if she could drown the ocean itself, she would. She would give anything for one more day with him.

"So you never learned?" he asked. His brows knit together.

"Like I said, he left when I was still a young girl."

"Well then," Flynn said, moving to the side of the helm. "It is never too late to learn, Princess."

Emily looked around as if he couldn't possibly be speaking to her, before setting her sights back on the pirate in front of her. "Right now?"

He shrugged his shoulders. "No better time than the present, or so I hear."

"Flynn...I don't think that's a good—" Flynn cut off her words as he reached for her arm and pulled her quickly towards him.

She stumbled forward and hit Flynn's chest. She looked up to him and he was already smirking.

Flynn spent the next few hours showing her how to read the compass and adjust their course accordingly. Admittedly, Flynn did have to step in a few times to correct an over turn. But by the time the sun had begun to set, Emily was comfortably steering the ship with little guidance from Flynn. He even let her use his compass.

However, she could feel his gaze on her, and without looking, she knew her own expression matched his. A blush crept onto her cheeks, and a soft smile spread across her face. Everything about that moment was peaceful.

"So," Flynn said from behind her. "What was it like growing up where you did? Why are women treated so differently?"

Emily looked down at the compass to confirm that she was on the right path before looking over her shoulders at Flynn. He was leaning against the wall with his arms crossed over his chest. His hair was still pulled back in that messy bun.

I wonder if he would let me braid it one day.

"I think that it has always been this way. I do not believe it will change either, at least not anytime soon. Women are sent to school to learn how to find a husband and how to be a *good* woman."

"And what is a *good* woman?"

"I guess...someone quiet? Well mannered. Someone who serves her husband and listens to his commands."

Flynn chuckled. "That does not describe you."

Emily's face turned even redder as she shot him a glare. He pushed himself off the wall and took two solid steps so that he was right beside her.

"How dare—"

Flynn grabbed her chin, turning her head to look directly at him as he leaned down to be eye level with her. "But if those qualities are what make a good woman, then I do not yearn for a good woman."

Emily opened and closed her mouth, but no words came out. She turned away from him and focused back on the sea, but she could still see him standing there next to her.

"I would like to one day visit whatever land you are from and usurp their ruler as well."

Emily scoffed as she shook her head. "If only it were that simple."

"It can be. Tell me where you are from."

"I told you already, Pirate, nowhere you would know."

"A princess from somewhere a pirate has never sailed before," he said from beside her. His hand moved a stray lock of hair behind her ear. "Sounds like an adventure."

Emily smiled. "And you would go with me on such an adventure if I asked you to?"

"I am afraid I would give up everything if you simply asked for it. And when this is all done, when the king is dead and the people are safe, perhaps we *can* go on an adventure."

Emily's smile fell for a moment. She tried to pass his comment off as a joke, but as she looked into his eyes, she could see his devotion. "An adventure of our own..." she began. Her smile returned as she leaned closer to him. "I am beginning to think that you may have actual feelings for me," she teased.

Flynn closed the distance between them with a tender kiss. Her eyes fluttered closed and she tried her best to engrave this moment into her memory. His touch, his scent, his presence, *everything*.

Flynn slowly pulled away and as she opened her eyes, he was staring down at Emily with a kindness reserved only for her. "If you think that I only might have feelings for you, then I have failed at making my intentions clear, Princess."

Emily's face heated as her mouth opened slightly, but no words were able to escape the barrier of her own heart. What was she to say to such a proclamation? She knew of course what she wanted to say.

'Then try harder to convince me to stay, Pirate. Kidnap me again. Make me yours.' But how could she? For now, she leaned in and kissed him again, silencing any chance for her to respond.

A FORGOTTEN LINE IN THE SAND

Emily

The right decision can often feel like the wrong one. Alternatively, the wrong decision can feel like the right one. Emily had let herself fall deeper into Flynn's world than she had ever intended to. She knew leaving was the only true option, but alas. The heart is a difficult thing to control. If you let it run free, it will break. And if you keep it locked away, it will cease to flourish in the wonders of the world. Though, such complexities make for a good story, dear reader. It is why you are still here, listening to me tell you this tale.

Emily quickly acclimated to life on the ship. The rocking of the boat and the call of birds above her was soothing in a way. It made her feel close to her father. She wondered if this is how he felt each time he left home, chasing a new adventure.

Her own adventure was fast approaching. From what Lucas had told her, they only had one more night before they reached Butchers Harbor. From there, at least from how the book went, Flynn would fail at getting a fleet of ships, but he would gain the loyalty of a few sailors who took pity on him. She didn't want Flynn to fail, of course not, but staying as close to the original story line would mean that she was set to return home after the death of the king. And, if the group of men he would gather meant his success and clean escape, then he would need to fail at his original plan first. Too much change could destroy more than just her chances of getting home. It could place Flynn in the direct path of danger.

She remained in the Captain's Cabin studying the maps. She couldn't make much sense of it herself, but she still wanted to try.

Maybe I can get Flynn to teach me before I leave.

He would probably be a good teacher. He taught her how to sail, after all. He was strict but kind. Thinking of how he might reprimand her made her heart quicken its pace. It had already been two days since he pleasured her. His touch was hungry and demanding yet, gentle. Since coming on the ship, and being so close to him, her desires only grew.

If her mother could see how unladylike she had become, she would surely faint.

Her own daughter gallivanting with a pirate. What a preposterous idea it was. And yet—Emily touched her lips, remembering the feeling of his mouth upon hers...and everything that came after—here she was.

A lady, not from his world, falling for a dastardly pirate. More than that, a lady who agreed to join him to usurp the current king. A lady who would leave him once she got to the end of his book. Emily ran her fingers over the splitting wood of the desk. The roughness of the wood raked against her skin.

"Even when I was reading the book in the Green Room,

it always felt so real..." She mumbled. Flynn was the most honest thing she had known for a very long time. He didn't waste time mincing words.

Emily walked over to the bed and fell back upon it. The softness of the sheets quickly enveloped her in a warm comfort. Yet, it still felt empty.

After knowing his touch, the remembrance of the feelings of both desire and want came to consume her thoughts. Like tasting sweetness for the first time.

I never even wanted to be around a man for longer than a night. Let alone open my heart to one.

But Flynn was different. He wasn't like the men in London. He did not care that she had her own thoughts or opinions, or that she was well read or could use a sword. In fact, he appeared to be drawn to that part of her. It was a rarity in and of itself.

He was rough and ragged and his hair was long and always tied back in a bun. He was rude and crass and even more than that, he was charming. Flynn was everything men in London were not.

Emily lifted her head up to glance at the closed door one more time.

The thought of Flynn's touch surfaced to her mind and she felt herself growing wet.

One more time and that's it.

She lifted up the skirt of her dress sending a thrill to her core as it dragged along her skin.

It's not right, I absolutely should not be doing this...

But her worries of being caught quickly melted away as her fingers found her clit.

Emily released a breath as her head fell back, letting her own hand bring her pleasure.

But each time the sensation of release began to bud, it disappeared leaving her moaning in frustration.

It's not enough.

When he had touched her he had reduced her to nothing but a moaning mess.

Emily kept teasing her sex with one hand, as the other moved lower towards the part that wanted Flynn the most.

As soon as her fingers thrust inside of her, electricity raced through her body.

"Yes," she whimpered.

She was so close.

"Flynn," she moaned.

But her voice was ripped from her as the handle to the door jiggled and without warning, slammed open.

NOT WITHOUT PUNISHMENT

Flynn

Two days had passed since he tasted her on his lips. It was not for a lack of effort, but every time he tried to steal a moment of her time, something required his attention. But each time his eyes searched for Emily, he found her already stealing glances at him with her doe eyes.

Each time their eyes met, he wanted nothing more than to drag her to the bed and fuck her until she was screaming his name. It would be the sweetest sound.

Perhaps bringing her was in all truth a bad idea. She was a distraction that he couldn't seem to be able to walk away from.

"Cap," Lucas said. He walked up from behind and clapped Flynn's shoulder. "I'll take over. We should reach Butchers Harbor by nightfall, so get some rest until then."

Flynn looked out at the open sea. The sun was still well above the horizon, but Lucas was right. He needed his wits about him. Once they reach Butchers Harbor, it would finally be time to make their first move.

Flynn stepped back from the helm letting Lucas take over. "Wake me if anything is amiss."

Lucas nodded and focused his attention on the ocean before them as Flynn turned and walked down the steps to the cabin. Below deck was quiet, and more importantly, private. If Emily were already asleep, he would be able to rest soundly next to her.

As Flynn reached for the door handle, he froze at the sound of a high-pitched whimper coming from inside the room. The sound of it pierced his core, causing his cock to harden in his pants.

He waited another moment, careful to not make a sound as his hand reached down to his pants and gripped his shaft, letting himself feel the slightest bit of release.

Any sense of restraint he had snapped when he heard another moan come from the room, sounding almost as desperate as he felt.

"Flynn," Emily called out.

Flynn turned the handle to the room and slammed open the door. Before him, sprawled out on his bed, was Emily. Her dress was pulled up, exposing her sex with her fingers thrust into her pussy. She shot up at the sound of the door and she quickly moved to cover herself.

"Oh my god!" she yelled as she pulled down her dress between her legs. "I-I am so sorry," Emily began. Her face was a bright red and her eyes watered as if she were about to be scolded, or worse, humiliated.

"Do not apologize, Emily."

"I shouldn't have—"

"Will you keep going?" he asked.

"What?" she breathed out. Her eyes finally left his to travel down his rigid body, landing on the hard bulge in his pants.

"Keep going, Emily, show me how you imagined me touching you." He stalked closer to her until his legs hit the edge of the bed. He moved his hand to cover his shaft and squeezed again.

Emily closed her eyes and nodded slowly as she laid back down, carefully lifting her dress with a pace far too slow for Flynn. Her fingers carefully began their ministrations, picking up pace once she found the spot that made her breath hitch.

His cock grew painful as her moans filled the room.

"Fuck yourself with your fingers, Emily. Imagine that it's my cock fucking you," he grit out, barely holding back the urge to reach forward and replace her hand with his.

Without hesitation, her fingers left her clit and dipped into her sex. She spread her legs wide as she came undone before him. Her fingers thrust rapidly in and out as her body tensed and release took over.

"Flynn!" she cried out. Her body shook slightly as her eyes opened again. She looked lost in a haze of pleasure. Her chest rose and fell with each deep breath.

Pride bubbled in him, mixing with a dark possession as he watched the mess she had become for him.

Emily's mouth hung open and her tongue darted out to wet her lips as she watched him. Slowly, she sat up and slid off the bed. His eyebrows furrowed at the thought of her trying to run away now, when all he wanted to do was stay in this room with her. However, when she lowered herself to her knees before him, and looked up at him with big pleading eyes, something sparked within his chest.

"Emily," he warned.

"I think..." Emily began, licking her lips, "that it is improper for a woman to display herself like that and maybe I ought to be punished..." Her voice trailed off as she looked at the bulge in his pants.

Fuck.

Flynn let out a low growl as he grabbed her chin with his free hand. He ran his thumb across her lips, parting her mouth slowly. Her tongue ran across his thumb and her eyes looked up at him with anticipation.

"Emily," he whispered.

She leaned forward and licked the outline of his cock, almost breaking every ounce of self-control he had. She moaned and her eyes fluttered shut for a moment before she held his gaze once more.

"So, it is punishment you want?"

HERS TO PLEASE

Emily

What am I doing?

She was practically begging him to punish her. It was like the only truth that existed between them right now was her need to submit and his desire to be her master. His cock was large enough that after licking up its length, even through his pants, Emily was nervous about her ability to take him into her mouth.

Flynn slowly removed his belt, discarding it to the side. He reached down, grabbed his cock and pulled it out, stroking himself a few times as he watched her with hungry eyes.

"Show me how much you wish to be punished."

Emily's tongue darted past her lips as she carefully licked the bead of cum running down the head of his cock. The taste of him spread across her lips and she could feel her desire begin to resurface. In their silence, she could hear Flynn take a sharp breath, causing her to smirk. Chancing a glance up, Emily's eyes lifted as she continued to lick and suck only his tip. When their eyes met, her stomach dropped.

Flynn's eyes darkened as his hands ran past the sides of her face to the back of her head, grabbing her by the hair and pulling her back so she could look at him fully.

"This is supposed to be a punishment, Emily. Open your fucking mouth."

A shudder raked down her back as Emily parted her lips. Flynn slowly thrust forward, his cock filling her mouth. A thrill of something sinful worked its way into her heart as his heavy cock pushed past her lips, hitting the back of her throat. She focused on breathing through her nose as her eyes watered, refusing to look away from him as she took her punishment like his good girl.

Without warning, he pulled back and thrust forward with a force that made Emily choke.

"That's it, Emily," Flynn grunted as he continued to fuck her needy mouth. "Take your punishment like the good princess you are."

Tears had begun to stream down Emily's cheeks as he continued to hit the back of her throat. When she started to think Flynn was becoming too much, Emily grabbed onto his legs for support.

"You can take all of me," Flynn panted, encouraging her to take him deeper down her throat. Even still, she couldn't take him deep enough to reach his base.

"You—" thrust, "—are" thrust, "—*mine*."

She should have felt embarrassed or ruined for any chance of marriage, but she felt freed and even more, she felt *wanted*.

The way he looked down at her with lust filled eyes only made her need for him run deeper.

"Good girl," he rasped.

It was the only warning she got before a hot liquid filled her mouth. He pulled away from her and pumped his cock rapidly, his seed spraying over her face and dripping down her lips. To her own surprise, she found her tongue darting out to catch more of him.

With each step Emily took closer to Flynn, she found herself surrendering new parts of herself to him.

And the most dangerous aspect of it all?

She enjoyed it.

Too much.

EMILY LAID AWAKE IN DARKNESS, the rocking of the ship lulling her uneasy mind into a calm state. She rolled onto her back and ran her hands down her face in frustration.

"What am I doing?" she mumbled to herself.

In just a few hours, they would arrive at Butchers Harbor. In a few days, they would kill the king. Once that happened, she was supposed to leave. She *would* leave...or at least she should.

But what awaited her back home? A marriage of convenience? A life as a kept wife?

Emily sighed and sat up, moving her legs to dangle over the edge of the bed. She looked across from her at the chair where Flynn slept soundly.

"What would the great Flynn Sawyer do if this were one of his adventures?" she whispered.

Guilt once again raked over her. Her mother was still home, unknowing of Emily's whereabouts. Most likely distraught at losing another person she loves. Yet, that was not the source of her guilt. It was her reason for returning home, that much was true. But what she was doing was beginning to untether her heart. She should be stepping back from Flynn, putting distance between them, but instead, she was taking steps closer to him. No part of her could say that it was because she needed his trust or his help to get home. It was because she *wanted* him.

Going home and leaving his world was the right decision, but it filled her with a sense of wrongness. On the other hand, staying here, with the promise of adventure, and perhaps even love, felt like a forbidden fruit being freely offered to her.

But would he accept her? Her being here was in and of itself an impossibility. And further, she had done nothing but lie to him with only bits of truth sprinkled in. All the while, she knew everything about his past and there was little he could hide from her.

Emily closed her eyes and fell back onto the bed. She pulled the covers tight over herself and released a breath.

If this were all some crazy dream, at least it would make everything easier. At least it wouldn't hurt so much.

She knew it would hurt him when she left, though at the very least, she hoped that he would not forget her entirely. She wanted to leave him with fond memories.

BUTCHERS HARBOR

Flynn

I personally believe that going some place where the forecast for death rises to fifty percent is not the wisest of choices. But when one is desperate enough, especially if it is for a just cause such as Flynn's, things like these can hardly be avoided.

Butchers Harbor was exactly as Flynn remembered. Smoke filled the dimly lit streets from fires lit by the townspeople. Outside each tavern was either an unconscious man or a dead one. Say the wrong thing to the wrong person and pray you end up as the former. It was home to some of the best thieves and assassins, and here, there was no honor among them.

Flynn and the group walked down the deck. He tossed a bag of coins to the harbor master and held up one finger. The older man nodded his head and pocketed the coin. Flynn made sure to throw in more coin than what was demanded for one night as incentive to keep his ship in one piece.

"Princess," Flynn called as he turned his head to look back over his shoulder. She was wearing a deep green dress that contrasted against her fair skin and reddish hair. His jaw tightened as he thought about what it would look like to rip it off her. She halted her conversation with Lucas who was only a step behind her to look up at Flynn. When their eyes met her cheeks began to redden. Flynn gestured for her to come stand beside him. "Stay close," he said softly. "And keep your head down."

Emily nodded as she walked beside him leaving Lucas and Levi to trail behind.

"I am capable of taking care of myself, Pirate." Emily's lips quirked up in a half smile. "Besides, shouldn't you keep *your* head down? What if you have a bounty on your head? You are practically a walking chest of gold."

Flynn caught her gaze and bit back a smile of his own.

"I guarantee I have a bounty. Everyone here does. If we were to all turn on one another, there would be no one left to run this harbor. In any case, I would like you to let me care for you while we are here. Is that asking too much, Princess? Am I being too forward?" he teased.

"I wouldn't mind if you were more forward," she whispered. She looked up at him through her long eyelashes and in that moment his heart felt like it was going to beat out of his chest.

She was a vision. She was the embodiment of kindness and beauty, and yet, she was also an enigma that he couldn't solve.

A girl from nowhere.

Flynn knew that she was not a psychic, but he also knew that there was a reason for her lying to him. She could be in danger. She could be running from someone. He did not care if everything she had told him up until now had been a lie, as long as she stayed by his side.

"Hey, Miss!" a man called from a foot away from them. A few men gathered behind the first. Each one looking like it had been years since their last bath. Emily and the group halted in their steps and turned to face the drunk men. "How about you come party with a real man?" he said, grabbing his crotch.

Flynn put his hand on his sword, but Emily grabbed his arm as she looked back at him, shaking her head.

"They are not worth it," she whispered.

Flynn released a breath and dropped his hold on his sword. He turned back to Levi and Lucas and nodded his head, motioning for them to follow.

They only made it a few steps before the man charged forward, this time yelling.

"Hey! I was talking to you, you bitch!" He brought his hand back and before anyone could react, he slapped Emily's ass and stepped back, laughing.

Flynn lunged towards the man, tackling him to the ground. His fist shot forward, connecting with the man's jaw with a distinctive crack. He hit him three more times before he realized both Levi and Lucas were trying to pull him off.

"Never," he shouted at the bloodied man, "lay your hands on her again."

The man rolled his head to the side, coughing up blood as he raised both of his shaking hands.

"I got it," he coughed, "I understand."

"You don't, but you will," Flynn whispered.

"Flynn!" Emily yelled. Flynn stood up and spat on the man. He backed away slowly and turned to face her. She looked scared, but not for the violence that had unfolded. Flynn's brows furrowed as he cocked his head to the side as

Emily rushed towards him. She grabbed both his hands in hers and examined his knuckles which were only scratched up.

She was scared for me.

Flynn couldn't stop the smirk from taking over his face. "Worried about me, Princess?"

Emily looked up at him with narrowed eyes, but quickly dropped his gaze to further examine his hands.

"Shit, Cap." Levi said. "Try and control yourself." As soon as the words left Levi's mouth, he paused shrugged his shoulders. "Never thought I would ever be the one saying that."

Flynn nodded his head towards Emily as he looked at Levi. "Take her to the inn safely, I will be right behind you in a moment."

"Flynn," Emily warned as Levi walked over to her, extending an elbow. "Do not hurt him. Just walk away."

She linked her arm with Levi who in turn patted her hand in what seemed to be a reassuring manner. Her eyes were hard set on Flynn until Levi began to lead her to the inn.

"I will not lay another hand on him, Princess."

Flynn watched as the two of them walked away. Half of the gathering crowd stepped out of the path after seeing what Flynn had done to the bloodied man on the ground. The other half kept their eyes trained on Emily.

It brought about a flame of possessiveness in his chest that he was not used to. Flynn rubbed his hand over his heart as if he could forcibly douse it.

But as he turned back around to look at the man on the ground, he knew there was only one way to smother his discomfort.

Coming here was dangerous, that much didn't escape

him. But he misjudged how much having Emily in the direct line of danger would affect him. And to think, such a disgusting man believed himself to be worthy of touching such a rare flower like Emily. Like his princess.

"Lucas," he said, not taking his eyes off the man. "Break the hand that he touched Emily with, and one rib for each finger on that hand. Don't worry about hiding him after the fact. I want them to know."

"Yes, Captain."

Flynn spun on his heels leaving Lucas to do the dirty work.

I said I wouldn't lay a hand on him. Never said anything about Lucas.

His steps on the cold stone seemed to echo as the once thriving port fell to a deathly silence after the scene he had caused. Flynn hardly made it ten steps before the first ear-piercing scream rang out. This time, no one's eyes were searching for the direction that Emily had gone off to. They were all on him and the live-action consequences of touching what was his.

That's right. Keep your eyes on me.

It was in all honesty better for the attention to be on Flynn. Tonight, he would meet with Blood Beard. Flynn's reputation was usually all he needed when meeting with either friend or foe, but Blood Beard was different. He held no true allegiances except to coin, which meant he was dangerous. A little buzz about the town would be sure to make Blood Beard aware of his presence. This harbor was not far off from Blood Beard's territory. If Flynn made his being here known, the older pirate would be less inclined to take it as a threat to his own armada.

Once Flynn reached the broken-down inn, that looked to be held together by nothing but hopes and prayers, he opened the door and walked in to see Levi and Emily already in talks with the innkeeper.

As the door clicked shut, Emily and Levi both turned to look at him. He didn't miss Emily's wary gaze as it traveled down his body to his hands. Flynn smirked as he held them up, showing that they were clean.

"I kept my word, Princess. I didn't lay a single hand on him."

"Where's Lucas?" Levi asked, eyeing the door.

Flynn shrugged his shoulders. "Said he wanted to meet the people here, you know how he is."

Levi narrowed his eyes at Flynn. His gaze slowly moved to Emily. A flash of understanding moved across his face and he shook his head slightly, barely hiding his smirk. "Ah yes, Cap," he said. "He is ever the charmer, isn't he? In that case, why don't I join him?"

"Sounds like a fine idea," Flynn said through a tight smile. He twisted his torso to the side to allow Levi to pass. Once the door was closed, the only sound to fill the room was the clinking of coins as the innkeeper tallied his earnings on his desk.

"So," the innkeeper said with a scratchy voice, "if yer done with the pleasantries, how many rooms and for how long?"

Flynn cleared his throat as he walked to stand beside Emily. He reached into his pocket and pulled out eight silver coins and slapped them onto the desk.

"What will this get me?" Flynn asked.

The man paused his counting to look at the coins, then up at Flynn. His judging gaze darted between Flynn and Emily before he sighed and bent down. The man opened up a drawer and rummaged through what sounded like metal before he fished out what he was looking for. He sat back up and haphazardly threw two keys onto the counter towards them.

"Two rooms," he grumbled before looking back down at his earnings. He continued stacking the coins into small piles, now incorporating Flynn's money.

"Two rooms?" Flynn asked. "Eight coins and I get two rooms?" The man didn't bother looking up from his pile of money. Flynn sighed as he picked up the keys which had room numbers etched into them. He slid them in his pocket as he wrapped his hand around Emily's waist and began leading her deeper into the inn. "Guess it's not only the townspeople that are thieves," he mumbled.

"It's four coins," the innkeeper grumbled.

They both stopped to turn back and stare at the innkeeper.

"What?" Emily asked.

The man sighed as he once again halted his counting. He looked up at Emily with amusement. "Two rooms, is four coins."

"But we paid—"

"And it's four coins for me to have never seen you around here before."

Emily looked up at Flynn, who mirrored her confusion before she turned back to the innkeeper. "I am not sure what impression we gave off, but we are in no need of your protection—"

"There are only two reasons a well-to-do woman like yourself comes around these parts," he said as he held up one finger. "One, she is running from something." He held up another finger. "Two, she plans on doing something that she would rather the Emerald Guard know nothing about. I do not care which it is. But if and when the Emerald Guard come snooping around, the extra fee is for me to have never seen you before. You, *Flynn Sawyer*," he said looking at Flynn, "are one of us. You have our silence while you are here. Some may even offer you their respect. But she is one of *them*. Her being here could put our own in danger."

Silence enveloped the group as his words sank in. Flynn glanced down at Emily. The innkeeper was right—she stood out like a sore thumb. Anyone would be able to tell she did not belong. They only just arrived and yet this is the second time someone has said something to her.

Flynn nodded his head towards the man. "We appreciate your discretion."

The innkeeper only waved them off as he resumed working.

Flynn placed his hand on Emily's back as he turned her around and led them to their rooms.

Flynn was toeing a dangerous line. One misstep and Emily could be harmed.

A SHOCKING REVELATION

Emily

"So what are you foreseeing for our stay here?" Flynn asked as he leaned against the wall to look out the window of the inn. Emily watched as he kept his eyes focused on the bustle of the town outside.

They would be sharing a room again tonight. Emily would be lying to herself if she were to say she wasn't at the very least relieved. She had become so used to Flynn's commanding presence that it would be hard to go back to being alone again like she was back home.

Having him around was equal parts exciting as it was frustrating.

"I told you," she said as she leaned against the door, facing Flynn. "It does not work like that. I know certain truths, but they do not come at random. What I can tell you, though, is that you will meet a pirate in hopes of gaining his fleet."

He glanced at her with a curious expression and raised eyebrows. "And the outcome of this is?" he asked, turning his body fully towards her while remaining against the window.

"If I tell you the outcome, it could change your course of events. And it's important to me that we get you to the king."

Flynn narrowed his eyes. "And why is that? What involvement have you in all of this?" He pushed off the wall and began walking towards her. "If it is not for revenge or justice, then what is it?"

She looked down at her feet as if they were more interesting than the current interrogation. But once Flynn's shoes stopped at the edge of hers, she slowly looked up, not stopping her eyes from roaming over his body. He was so close that she had to crane her neck back slightly.

"Why do you want to help me, Princess?"

Her eyes danced between his and she swallowed thickly.

"I—" she started.

"Please, Emily. I know so very little about you, outside of your father and the abandoned marriage proposal," he said with a bit of a bite at the end. As if telling her she would never see the day where she would stand at an alter next to a man she didn't know just to keep a house. "You stay so guarded. At least tell me this much," he asked softly.

Her stomach dropped at his plea. He was right. She did know almost everything there was to know about him after reading his book over and over again. She knew his struggles and insecurities, and the whole reason for going on this mission in the first place. Yet, all she was to him was a girl from nowhere.

What would he say if she told him the truth? Would he pull away from her completely? Emily shook her head slightly. "I will," she finally said. "I will tell you everything, just not yet."

She tried to look down again, but Flynn caught her chin in his hand and gently lifted it up as he brought his lips down upon hers.

He pulled back slightly so their noses brushed against one another.

"Then at least tell me one thing about yourself, even if it is small...like something you enjoy," he whispered.

"I love reading," she responded.

Flynn smiled as he leaned back down and kissed her once more, rewarding her for her honesty.

Emily melted into his kiss, wrapping her arms around his neck to pull him down closer.

Flynn's tongue traced her bottom lip and she gladly opened her mouth for him. Their tongues danced together as he grabbed her thigh with a firm grip and lifted it to be against his hip.

Flynn gently broke away to trail kisses down her neck. Each press of his lips and bite upon her was like fire coursing through her body.

"Flynn..." Emily said in a breathless moan.

A knock sounded at the other end of the door causing Emily to startle, but Flynn held her tight in place, his lips barely leaving her body.

She angled her head towards the door, listening for whoever might be on the other side.

"Ignore it," came Flynn's rough voice as he bit her neck. Emily gasped at the sensation of his teeth raking against her skin.

The knock came again, this time followed by Levi's voice. "I'm not leaving so it will be easier to open up, Cap. It's time, aye?"

Flynn groaned against her skin as he carefully dropped her leg and pulled away from her, leaving her a slightly pink and disheveled mess. He dropped her heated gaze to look at her fully. He smirked as he shamelessly adjusted himself in his pants, attempting to hide his want for her.

Emily's face reddened even further. She quickly fixed her dress as best as she could before shooting Flynn a knowing glare.

"Pirate," she mumbled.

"Princess," he responded, crossing his arms over his chest as he smirked.

Emily stumbled to open the door, revealing Levi leaning against the frame with a cat like grin, while Lucas stood against the wall across from them with his usual stoic look. But when his eyes settled on her, his expression softened as he nodded his head.

"Miss," Lucas said.

"Hope we were not interrupting much," Levi added, his grin only broadening.

Flynn took Emily's hand in his own as he came to stand beside her, ignoring Levi completely. "Are you ready, Princess?" he asked, looking down at her.

"As I'll ever be." She gave his hand a reassuring squeeze as they walked out into the hallway, letting the door close behind them. The walk from the hallway to door leading outside was short, the entire inn must have only consisted of a handful of rooms, and at most one dining area.

When they walked out into the street, darkness had fully set in. Flynn kept a firm grip on her waist which must not have been easy due to his height, but he never once let her go. She followed beside him as Levi and Lucas both trailed closely behind.

This town was so entirely different from Dardurin. Men laid about drunk in the streets, and more than a few men fought with one another, staining some areas of the road red with blood. Emily kept her back straight as she continued beside Flynn.

She looked up at him and a shadow of guilt washed over her. He was trying so hard to gather men to fight along side him, but upon requesting help from Blood Beard, he would be swiftly turned away for lack of coin. That didn't mean no one would help. Flynn would still gain the assistance of a few lost sailors. But the fact that she had to walk along side him on his way to be turned down, sat heavy in her heart.

Flynn squeezed her waist as they approached a large beaten down tavern with the name Deadman's Locker posted across the front. The roof looked caved in and the smells coming from inside was of pure ale, to the point that it was almost overwhelming. All the grass outside of the tavern looked trampled on, and even the walls themselves looked to be built out of splitting wood.

"Stay close to me," Flynn said as he reached for the handle and opened the door.

As soon as they walked inside they were met with a rowdy crowd of men, some locked in arm wrestling matches, some playing cards, all while others screamed for more ale.

But it was what remained at the back of the tavern that caught Emily's attention. Her heartbeat picked up pace as Flynn guided her through the masses of drunken men pushing against one another.

Emily kept her eyes trained on the tall man facing away from her at the end of the tavern. He sat at a round table with multiple pirates surrounding him, most likely his immediate crew members.

Once they were behind him, his crew members eyed the group and nodded their heads as if to signal to Blood Beard that he had company.

Blood Beard sighed as he righted himself. He wore what looked to be an old sailor's jacket. His hair was dark brown peppered with white. As he straightened himself, Emily could tell that he must have been tall, maybe even as tall as Flynn.

"Blood Beard," Flynn began. His voice was drenched with command and confidence as he addressed the rogue pirate before them. "I have come bearing a proposition. It involves over throwing the Emerald King."

"Not interested," Blood Beard said. Emily's eyebrows rose at the deep voice. He sounded gruff and...lost.

"If you would offer me a moment of your time, I promise to make it worth your while. We have brought plenty of coin."

Blood Beard scoffed as he took a sip of ale out of his mug. He set it down on the table with a loud thud, causing some of the drink to splash over the sides.

"All of the coin in that castle could not convince me to be a part of any usurpers plans."

"People are suffering, and we must make a stance," Flynn pushed. His grip grew tighter on her waist and his voice began to grow rough around the end.

"I hold no ties to either side of this stance you speak of. I simply ride each wave as it comes, *never* looking back."

"This is not something that you can walk away from, as a man—" Flynn was cut off by the scraping sound of Blood Beard pushing his chair back to stand fully.

He whipped around causing his own men to place their hands on their blades, waiting for his command.

"As a man, what?" he said as he turned to face Flynn.

Emily looked at Blood Beard and her mouth fell open. Without warning, a single tear slid down her face. Her reaction caused Blood Beard to turn and look at her.

When their eyes met, his expression quickly mirrored her own.

Blood Beard reached for Emily, but this time Flynn was not late in pulling her away. He grabbed her waist and pulled her back, locking her in place tightly against himself as he drew his sword. Blood Beard's men followed suit, aiming their own swords at the group. Levi and Lucas rushed to Flynn's side, weapons at the ready.

"No!" Emily yelled. "Don't!"

Blood Beard narrowed his eyes at Flynn before he looked down at where he held Emily in place.

His eyes darkened as his voice boomed through the once noisy tavern.

"Unhand my daughter."

FIRST IMPRESSIONS

Flynn

A hush fell upon both the armed men and Flynn's group.

"Daughter?" Flynn asked.

"Unhand her or I will break every bone in your body, *pirate scum*," Blood Beard spat.

Emily pushed against Flynn's hands and he looked down at her struggling against his grip. She looked up at him with tear filled eyes, and damn him. He let her go.

She immediately rushed over to Blood Beard and threw herself in his arms. He wrapped her in a tight embrace and —Flynn could have sworn—his eyes were also glistening. Blood Beard pet the back of Emily's head as she cried into his shoulders.

"Oh, my sweet girl..." he repeated over and over again, holding Emily as if she would disappear if he let go.

Flynn watched in amazement at the sight unfolding before them. Questions raged through his mind but none of them he had answers for. Flynn gestured for his men to put away their weapons.

Levi leaned in towards Flynn, placing a hand on his shoulder.

"She's Blood Beard's kid? Would explain the swordsmanship. Maybe he sent her for you," he whispered.

Flynn's expression, as well as his heart, dropped. Since the fire festival, he had been trying to figure out how she knew so much about him. Was this it? Was everything a lie? Did Blood Beard send his daughter for Flynn?

He lifted his gaze back to Emily to where she was still embracing her father.

Blood Beard placed a gentle kiss on the top of her head. "My sweet girl, what are you doing here?"

Emily leaned back slowly, but Blood Beard still held her shoulders. She used the back of her hands to wipe away the freely falling tears.

"Me? You...you're alive!" she said with a shaken voice. "I thought you were dead. I thought I would never see you again!" She hugged him once more and Blood Beard once again held her close.

Flynn watched as Emily's body shook as she cried softly into Blood Beard's shoulder.

"I never thought the day would come that I would see what a beautiful woman you have turned out to be," he said softly.

What Flynn was seeing, a man torn by grief over what he can only assume was the loss of time and years with his daughter, was not the merciless pirate he had come to hear stories about over the years.

Something about their relationship unsettled him. If he didn't die, and he wasn't held captive, why didn't he go back to Emily? One can fake many things, but the look on Blood Beard's face was of pure agony.

Why couldn't you go back to her?

Emily whispered some more words of relief and Flynn did not attempt to interrupt until she pulled away from Blood Beard. He watched as she turned her head, looking back at Flynn with dried tears on her cheeks. "There is someone I think you need to meet," she said to her father. "I know you already told him no, but Father, this is very important to me as well. Even if it is just for me, please, speak with him."

Flynn couldn't tell how he was supposed to feel. Emily was putting her own neck on the line to help him in his mission. Flynn bowed his head to Blood Beard.

If this is how I am meeting her father, I have to show that I am worthy of his daughter.

He lifted his head to meet Blood Beard's eyes, but the older pirate only glared back at Flynn.

"You have raised a determined daughter," Flynn complimented.

Blood Beard nodded his head. His eyes darted between Emily and Flynn.

"It seems I have," he relented. "Let us speak alone, then."

"Emily is free to hear what I have to say," Flynn argued.

"I do not think you will want that. Are your men good men?" Blood Beard asked, eyeing Levi and Lucas.

"They would lay down their lives to keep any one of us safe. Including your daughter. They are more than good men."

Blood Beard nodded, and dropped his hands from Emily. "Then have them escort her to her room and keep her safe while we discuss matters privately."

"Of course," Flynn relented. Emily walked over to him and Flynn gently grabbed her face with his hands to wipe away her tears. Her wet eyes looked up to him and he felt like he held the world in his hands. He leaned in and kissed her forehead softly. "Wait for me in the room, I will not be long, Princess."

Emily didn't respond, she only nodded her head and walked towards Levi and Lucas who each offered her their elbow as they escorted her out of the tavern. Blood Beard's men followed suit and one by one abandoned the tavern. It was only after they had left that Flynn noticed that all of the patrons had left as well, and it was only the two of them that remained. Flynn was well known as a skillful pirate. But Blood Beard was known for his rage. They probably left in a haste thinking they might be next.

When Flynn turned back to Blood Beard, he was met with not a pirate, but a protective father. Arguably worse.

"I have kept her safe, I swear it. I would die before I let anyone hurt her."

"You are a good man. I assume that fight in the port earlier was you keeping her safe?"

Flynn straightened his posture and gave a stiff nod. "Thank you, sir. And yes. I did not let him walk away without punishment."

"Like I said, a good man. Which is why I must thank you for returning my daughter to me." He reached behind him and grabbed his mug of ale, pointing it at Flynn. "I will offer you my armada. They are at your disposal and command."

"Thank you, sir, I cannot express enough how much good this will do when I kill the king. Our people will be free of his—"

"Yes, yes. Very good," he said as he waived away what

Flynn was saying. "Just make sure you say good bye to Emily before you leave. She is sentimental, you see."

His eyebrows quirked up. "Goodbye? What do you mean?" he asked carefully.

"Well, you have brought me my daughter. As payment, I will grant you what you ask for. In turn, you will leave her out of your world." Blood Beard initially watched Flynn with a blank expression, but then his eyes widened with realization. After a moment, he shook his head slightly, a hint of amusement playing at his lips.

"Did you think that a pirate like yourself could ever actually give her a decent life? Do you think I do not recognize you, Flynn Sawyer? Half of my men, at some point, have had a run in with you. It is hard to not recognize someone with such a tale to tell. Especially not with nearly all ports decorated with ink sketches of your face. Let me ask you, what happens after the king is dead? Hm? Will you, a pirate, take his place? No. You will be baiting the whole of the Emerald Guard into hunting you down. And what if someone worse takes the king's place?" He shook his head. "That is no life for my daughter."

Flynn shook his head as he took a step closer to Blood Beard. "I will give her a good life. Everything she could ever want, I will give it all to her. I am sorry, but I cannot leave her side."

Blood Beard sighed as he set down his drink. He leaned back against the table, crossing his arms over his chest. "I see that you are a man with honor. But deep down you must recognize that she is different than you, than the people here. She is not part of this world. Sooner or later, you will have to let her go. And if you truly care for her, then I would hope you would see that it is for the best."

Blood Beard took one final chug from the mug of ale

before setting it down harshly on the table. Flynn stood in silence, not moving an inch as Blood Beard walked past him, clapping him twice on the shoulder before making his way out of the empty tavern.

Flynn stayed in that tavern, alone, trying to recall what life was like not long ago before he first met his girl from nowhere, kneeling in the middle of Oakden.

Why had he taken her? Did he ever actually believe she was the king's daughter? Or did he recognize the look of being lost and lonely, marred across her face as the same one he had come to recognize in the mirror?

Am I truly selfish for not wanting to live in that loneliness anymore?

If wanting to keep her by my side makes me a selfish man, then I will become the epitome of possessiveness in my desperation to keep her.

A PHANTOM OF GUILT

Emily

Life and love are both fleeting. They stay for glorious moments and are ripped from us the next. It is why when you have them, you must cherish them entirely.

Emily sat on the edge of the bed staring out the window to the darkened town. How many impossibilities have happened since she arrived? And now the grandest of them all; her father lives. She didn't know what to feel. When he had turned around, she thought she was seeing a ghost. It had been years since he had vanished, years since she had come to terms with his death.

And my mother...my mother is alone. But unlike me, she never lost hope that he was alive.

Her heart felt like it was stuck between two opposing storms; one joy at this revelation, the other heartache at the thought that all these years, the pirate that Flynn had tried to win over, was her father. But as she looked back on the story, Blood Beard's description did sound like her father. But how was she to ever believe that her father had fallen into a world of fiction when he disappeared? She would have been considered mad for even having such a thought.

But...if he was in the book, and I read about it...that means that we alter the story as a whole. My presence is most likely being recorded. Everything I do, will affect the story.

Even if she were to dissect whatever emotions towards Flynn that she may or may not have, if she were to act on them anymore than she already has, it could change the course of events even further than it already has. Just by asking her father for help she was altering how Flynn over-throws the king. Still, she could not just say nothing and leave her father here.

The door behind her closed with a click, pulling her from her thoughts as she whipped around to the source of the sound. Flynn walked over to her with a look of bitterness on his face. His eyes were sunken and distant. But when his gaze finally met hers, his expression softened and he offered her a smile that didn't quite reach his eyes.

Emily quickly shot up and rushed over to Flynn, grabbing his hands in her own. Her eyes searched his for any indication of what had transpired between him and her father, but they were empty of anything but his attention and affection towards her.

He leaned down and kissed her forehead tenderly.

"Are you alright, Princess?" he asked.

"I am...in shock. I believe, at the very least..." she said as she pulled one of her hands from his and flicked it about in front of her face as if to wave some sense into herself. "All these years, and I never once held hope that he was alive and yet, he is. My mind feels as though it has been plunged beneath the crashing waves at sea...I'm so thrown about by it all that I am not even sure which way is up right now," she said, her voice beginning to crack. "But I need to speak with him. I...I never thought I would have another chance at seeing him again so I don't even know what I should say."

He dropped her other hand and lifted his own to cup the sides of her face.

"You do not always have to be perfectly put together, you are allowed to feel cracked once in a while. And," he continued, "anything you say will be enough."

Emily released a breath and closed her eyes, letting herself focus on the things directly around her. She could hear the waves in the distance, chatter from outside that had been slowly dying out, the sound of Flynn's even breaths, and his rough yet gentle touch upon her.

She opened her eyes again, immediately finding his gaze upon her. His eyes darted between hers as if he were searching.

"Do you want to ask me something?" she asked.

He shook his head slightly, relaxing his melancholy features.

"It can wait," he whispered.

HER FATHER HAD BEEN WAITING for her just outside of the inn when she had left Flynn. She couldn't help but think of the pained expression on his face, and his practiced-plastered on-kind-hearted smile. It was almost enough to make her want to turn back, to tell him everything. But would she believe someone if they told her that her life was just a book?

Even when she met Flynn for the first time, he had thought her to be daft or drunk.

Emily chuckled slightly at the memory of that cold night as she walked along side her father.

"He seems like a good man," her father said.

Emily straightened her back as she looked at him. They stopped walking and she came to stand in front of him.

"And you," he began, tucking a loose strand of hair behind her ear. "Look at how much you have grown. You look just like your mother." His eyes glistened under the moonlight with unshed tears as he spoke. "How is she?"

Emily smiled as she wiped away her own tears that were beginning to blur her vision.

"She misses you so much. She prays for you every single night. Not a day goes by that she is not talking about you."

"I miss her so much, my heart stopped beating the day I left her."

"What happened the night you disappeared?"

He shrugged his shoulders. "Can't say I remember much of the whole thing. One moment, I'm working with my crew to break through a storm, the next," he gestured around them. "I wake up here, on the beach of Butchers Harbor. Alone. None of my crew made it out, or at least ended up with me. It took me until I heard the name Flynn Sawyer, a year or so in, to realize that I was in the book I planned to give you. I only skimmed the pages so I had no way of knowing what my life would look like. As the years passed, any hope I had of going home slowly dissipated. So, I made the most of it. I moved forward, never looking back."

Emily listened to every word her father said, waiting for a few moments of silence to set in before she spoke.

"Did you ever think to seek Flynn out? Maybe he could have been of help?"

Her father looked at her with kind eyes. "I came here years ago. Flynn was only just beginning his story at the time. Besides, have you told Flynn who you really are? Where you are from?" She looked down, trying to hide the guilt that had begun to surface. He glanced back at the inn and sighed. He turned back to face Emily with almost a knowing look. "What use would he have been, if me being here was an impossibility? But that pirate of yours, has he treated you right? How did you two meet?"

Emily tried her best to fight her smile as she recalled him thinking she were a princess and had gone so far as to kidnap her. But seeing the reputation her father had built here, she also knew to leave a few bits out.

"He has kept me safe. He was the one who found me when I first arrived. I felt so lost and he was the first one to offer me a hand. He took me home to his island and his people accepted me with open arms, they made me feel at home."

"Mhm," her father acknowledged her words, but did not interrupt her story, beckoning her to continue.

"He does not know I am not from here. I am still trying to figure out the right way to tell him."

"Do you care for this man?" he asked her.

She nodded her head, hoping the darkness would hide her blush. "Like you said, he is a good man."

"But do you care for him, Emily. Do you love him?" This time his voice was more firm.

"I..."

"You cannot stay here, Emily. This is not our world. This is not our home. I have someplace here that is safe, away from this violent part of the world. He is a pirate—"

"So are you," she blurted out.

"Yes. That is exactly why I know that he will never be able to give you a life in which you are not in constant danger." He released a breath, and evened out his voice, letting his shoulders drop from their tense state. His clothes were so different from what she was used to seeing him in.

Gone was the formally dressed tradesman, replaced by a rugged pirate dressed in luxury fabrics with multiple guns hanging across his chest. "I have finally found you," he continued, "I will not lose you again, especially not to a battle that is not your own."

She understood what her father was saying, but his words picked away at her heart piece by piece, nonetheless.

"Your mother must be worried sick," he added.

"Well," Emily cleared her throat as she looked up at him. "When you come home, I fear she will never let you go again."

Her father's eyes fell as he looked at her. "Emily..." he began, "I have been searching for a way home for the last ten years. I didn't believe that I was the first to come here so I thought if I could find someone like me, a person not from this world, I might also find a way back. Yet after years of searching, I found no one. Not even a single crew member of mine from when I left our world. There is no way home."

"But there is! At least I think so."

He looked skeptical, but he kept listening.

"Every book has an end," she began, "nothing after that. I believe if we are able to get Flynn to kill the king, the story will come to its natural end and we will be sent back home." She tried her best to ignore the guilt that began to bubble in her chest. "But we must stay with him until the very end."

He sighed and took her hands gently in his. He stared down at her, letting silence fall upon them.

She wasn't a psychic, but she knew what he was thinking. She had been thinking it, too. What if she were wrong, what then? Then her mother would be left completely alone. But they could not allow themselves to drown before they even try to make it to the surface.

"We have found each other," she said, looking up at him.

He lifted his head and met her gaze with heavy eyes. "We have to try."

"You will come home with me as well. We will finally be a family again."

He pulled her into a strong embrace. Emily wrapped her arms around him as her eyes searched for the inn where she left Flynn.

"Yes," she whispered. "A family."

NOT WILLING TO SAY GOODBYE

Flynn

The door to the inn closed with a soft click. Flynn could hear quiet shuffling across the floor boards and he couldn't stop the smirk from appearing on his face at the thought of Emily trying not to wake him. He rested flat on his back with his arms behind his head. He kept his eyes closed, waiting for Emily to lay next to him.

The bed dipped slightly under her as she climbed onto the mattress and slipped under the covers. But when he did not feel Emily snuggling against him, he peeked one eye open to see that she was teetering on the edge of the bed.

Flynn let out a deep sigh as he rolled onto his side, propping his head up on one of his hands as he used the other to grab Emily by the waist and pull her away from the edge and flush against him.

Emily shrieked and whipped her head back to face him, her eyes were wide and her plump lips were slightly parted.

He leaned down and placed a tender kiss upon her forehead. "If you are uncomfortable sharing a bed, Princess, I can sleep on the floor. It's good for the back."

Emily smiled and shook her head, seeming to hold back a laugh.

"No...I am not uncomfortable. It's just," she paused, and looked up at him through her eyelashes. Even in the darkness he knew that her cheeks were painted red. Emily grabbed the blankets and pulled them over her head to hide herself. Flynn laughed and tried to pull the blankets off of her but she kept her grip firm.

He sighed as he rested his arm over her torso, giving her the privacy she seemed to want. Although his more possessive side did not like the idea of her shying away from him.

"It's because," she began. Her voice was muffled by the sheets. "Last time you warned me about what would happen if we shared a bed..."

"Last time?" he muttered, mainly to himself.

This time, his own cheeks heated with embarrassment as he recalled the time from the Captain's Cabin where he had warned her about what sharing a bed would do to him.

"Ah Princess, I—"

"But I feel stupid. I mean we have done other things, but doing *that* with *you* makes me so nervous. It's not like I have no experience but—" she was speaking so fast her words began to trip over themselves.

"Princess," he said again, this time more firm, halting her ramblings. "I want you more than anything else. This is true. But I want more than just your body. Even *I* know there is a time and place. You have had a trying day. We both have. I promise I only wish to hold you while we sleep. And you never need to explain yourself to me. If you say we stop, we stop. I am yours to control, yes?"

He let his hand mindlessly caress her covered form, hoping to comfort her.

"But if this makes you uncomfortable," he continued, "then I will gladly sleep on the floor, or better yet, kick Levi out of his room. God knows he has probably broken the final tether that holds Lucas' patience."

Emily laughed from under the blanket, causing the sheets to jiggle with her movement. She slowly pulled the blanket down just enough to reveal her doe eyes.

"What do you want me to do, Princess?"

"I want you to hold me while I sleep," she whispered.

Flynn nodded his head as he laid back on the bed. He scooped Emily up and pulled her against his side. Her head rested on his chest as Flynn lazily traced lines up and down her arm until her breath slowly evened out.

If he could describe heaven, this would be it. Even if this moment was fleeting, he wanted to cherish every second of it. But as Flynn lay awake in the darkness, he couldn't get Blood Beard's words out of his mind.

He angled his head down so that he could gaze at Emily as she slept soundly, safe and protected by him.

"Say goodbye?" he whispered as he placed another kiss on the top of her head. "Never."

THE SUN BEAT down on Flynn and his crew as they all loaded up onto Blood Beard's main ship. It was immensely larger than Flynn's, and was battle ready. It was exactly what he needed. Cannons lined either side of the ship. It looked to house at least fifty crew members and even some cooks. Blood Beard himself was already waiting at the helm.

They spent much of the morning packing up maps and

the necessary items from Flynn's ship, and transferring it over to Blood Beard's.

It had come as a shock when Blood Beard had told Flynn that he would help deliver him to the king. Still, beneath his promise to be an ally, he knew that his threat to take Emily away from him still existed.

I will not let that happen.

Emily walked past Flynn carrying a bag. He reached out and pulled the straps back, causing her to fall against him. Her back was pressed against him and he brought his hand under her chin to lift up her smiling face. He leaned down and kissed her, burning her taste and touch into his memory.

When he let her go, she lowered her head and turned around, smiling with rose-colored cheeks.

"Come on," she said, extending her hand to him.

I must have been a saint in my past life. Maybe I saved a village.

Flynn took her hand and they began to board the ship. But his smile faded into a scowl as he looked back up to the helm only to find her father staring down at them with his arms crossed over his chest like he was their prison ward.

Or who knows. Maybe I burned one down and this is some sort of hellish punishment.

Flynn dropped her father's gaze only to bring his focus back to the only thing worth his attention— her. He squeezed her hand as they walked onto the ship and in that moment, he knew that not even the god of death would be able to make him let her go. He loved her dangerously, viciously, and beautifully.

I can protect her.

They moved across the deck towards the helm where her father was waiting, passing by crew members, cooks and crooks alike. They walked up the stairs to stand before her father. Blood Beard's scowl remained plastered on his aging face, overflowing with disappointment.

"Emily," he said. "Flynn and I must discuss the battle plans so why don't you—"

"Stay." Her words rang out with finality. She looked at Flynn then back at her father. "Father," she began, "there is much we all need to discuss. I am just as much apart of this as you are now. I will stay, and we will all work together. It is the only chance we have at defeating the king. We need to work as a unit."

Footsteps approached behind them and Flynn angled his head back to see a cheerful Levi and only partially annoyed Lucas walking up behind them.

Lucas nodded his head towards Emily as he crossed his arms over his chest.

"She is right, Sir." Lucas said to Blood Beard. "With all due respect, I do not see many women aboard this ship, and if we are to succeed in infiltrating the ball, Flynn will need a date with knowledge on the upper class."

"What he means to say," Levi cut in, throwing his arm over Lucas' shoulders. Lucas looked away but made no attempt to move. Flynn smirked and looked back towards Blood Beard who was still eyeing Levi with a look of mistrust. "Is that after you abandoned your daughter, she was already set to marry a lord of your lands. She will blend in with the rich. After all, who would expect a princess to be in arms with a pirate?"

Blood Beards eyes widened as he looked at Emily. "What are they talking about?"

"You didn't know?" Flynn asked. He squeezed Emily's hand again and ran his thumb over her knuckles. She peered up at Flynn and he nodded his head. She looked back to her father and for the first time, Flynn actually felt bad for him. He looked as if his heart was breaking.

"Father...you were gone for a long time. You know the law. After some time, they told us we only had a few more months before they took the house. Mother is trying to save what little she has left of you."

"Did you agree to this?" Her father asked.

"What choice did I have?"

Blood Beard sighed as he ran his hand down his face, seeming to rub away the pained look.

"Well then, Flynn Sawyer, let's get to work."

A PLAN IN MOTION

Flynn

The Captain's Cabin aboard Blood Beard's ship was far larger than expected, with a table that took up the middle of the room. There was even a wall dividing the meeting area from the sleeping quarters. Flynn noticed the touches of red and gold throughout Blood Beard's ship, boasting his preferences for the bold colors. The entire ship was well decorated and painted even on the inside.

It almost made Flynn feel embarrassed about the ship he had spent so much time on with Emily.

They all piled into the room, yet even with all five of them in the same space, the cabin was not even close to feeling like a tight squeeze.

"So," Blood Beard began as he closed the door behind him. He walked over to the table until he could lean over it. "What is your grand plan? Hm? How will we kill the Emerald King?"

Lucas dropped the crate he was carrying onto the floor. He leaned down and pulled out a rolled-up map and carefully set it on the table. He held the edge of the paper down and rolled out the map, using a few old mugs to weigh down the corners.

The map outlined the island where everything would be taking place. It was small and full of rocky terrain.

Flynn pointed to the mountains drawn behind the castle. "We needn't worry about an attack from behind. The mountains will make our path rather straight forward."

"It will also make our chance for escape narrow," Levi added. "Once in the office, I will make sure we have a backup escape just in case the front doors are occupied."

"But with your fleet and men," Lucas began, "we should be able to surround them on most fronts. There will be some guards watching the ships, but nothing that we won't be able to handle. The real trouble comes when we get inside the ball."

"And what is your plan for when you make it inside?" Emily's father asked.

"That's where Emily comes in," Flynn interjected, "she will pose as my date and I will be taking on the identity of Isaac Bensworth. Fifth—"

"Grandchild to the Duke of Oshwire?" Blood Beard finished. He shrugged his shoulders. "I would have gone with someone less flashy, but I guess it suits your taste."

"Well, someone less flashy would not have been able to gain an invitation. Besides, we are similar in age and looks, keeping our deception as close to the truth as possible will result in less questions being raised."

Blood Beard scoffed. "You have a recognizable face, what's your plan for that?"

Emily placed her hand on Flynn's shoulder, giving it a slight squeeze. "It will be a masquerade ball," she started. "Everyone will be wearing a mask, myself included."

Her father tensed as she spoke. Making sure to glare at Flynn the entire time. "Is your attendance necessary, Emily?"

Flynn stepped forward. "Her attendance will ensure the believability of—"

"I am not asking you, Pirate," Blood Beard spat.

Flynn scoffed. "Last I checked you're a pirate too, arguably worse than me—"

"Right then!" Emily said, clapping her hands in front of her. "We need this to go off smoothly," she said, making sure to look each and every one of them in the eyes.

Emily let her gaze finally fall onto her father. "For all our sake. I need to be there when Flynn meets the king, and once this is all over, Father, we will meet back here on this ship."

"We might need help from your men securing the area," Flynn sighed. "Emily will remain by my side, *protected*, the entire night as my date. Levi and Lucas will have their own masks and pose as servers."

Blood Beard stared down at the map. Silence fell upon the group as they waited for his answer.

Flynn didn't like having to work with him any more than Blood Beard did. But this was about more than them. He needed a way to convince her father that not only would he keep Emily safe during the ball, he would keep her safe always. He hated to admit it, but without his trust, they would get nowhere.

Flynn sighed as he dropped his head. He took a moment to gather his thoughts before he finally straightened his body and reached down to take Emily's hand in his own. Right away Flynn could see out of the corner of his eye, Blood Beard was no longer looking at the map.

Emily looked up well as Flynn brought her delicate hand to his lips and placed a soft kiss atop her fingers.

His eyes held her soft gaze for a moment before motioning his head towards her father, hoping she would catch his implication. Thankfully, she smiled and nodded. It was all the permission his princess needed to grant him.

Flynn let her hand fall from his lips, taking away her sweet scent and softness with it. He looked back at Levi and Lucas and cleared his throat.

"Blood Beard and I must discuss things in private. Please busy yourselves with helping the crew and we will find you when we are finished."

"Aye," Levi said carefully as he took a step back. Lucas followed suit and they both slowly made their way out of the quarters. Most likely not trusting Flynn or Blood Beard for that matter to keep their tempers under control.

"Behave," Emily said as she walked towards the door. She looked over her shoulder one last time. Her eyes darted between the two of them. "Both of you," she added.

"As you wish, Princess," Flynn said through a smirk. As she left, he could make out the slightly red tint that brushed her cheeks.

The door closed behind her leaving Flynn and his soon to be—whether the old man liked it or not—father-in-law alone in the cabin.

When Flynn brought his focus back to Blood Beard, the other man's features were already hard set.

How did a wild boar raise a gentle doe?

"I know that you are worried—"

"You know nothing," Blood Beard cut in. "I have only just found her again and you are asking me to send her away, directly into danger. She is my only daughter. I lost her once, Flynn, you will not be the reason I lose her again."

"I may not be able to understand as a father, but as a man, I do. I promise you if it ever came down to her life or my own, I will protect her and lay down my life so that she may take another breath."

Blood Beard shook his head, avoiding Flynn's eyes as he looked back down at the map with his hands braced against the table.

"May I ask you something?" Flynn asked.

"Because you haven't asked enough?"

Flynn ignored his comment. "Why couldn't you go back to her? You don't seem like the kind of man to willingly abandon his daughter and leave her to be married off like cattle."

Blood Beard lifted his head to glare daggers at Flynn. "Watch your tongue!"

"Or what? What words am I speaking that are untrue? Why did you not go back?"

"It is complicated."

"Then help me understand," he asked firmly.

Blood Beard let out a deep breath as he lifted himself to stand upright. He shook his head again, this time as if he were looking for an answer. "This is not my truth to tell. But you must understand, you and her do not belong in the same world. No matter how much you say you care for her, she will always be in danger if she is with you." Blood Beard walked around the table to stand in front of Flynn. He raised both of his hands and placed them on Flynn's shoulders. "I am begging you, as a man, as her father, when this is over, I need you to do the right thing and send her home. It is the only way she will ever be safe. If you truly want to protect my daughter, tell her to go home."

Flynn's brows knit together as guilt and anger molded into one, sinking deep into his chest. His eyes danced between Blood Beard's desperate ones. He could not bring himself to lie.

"I can't let her go."

Blood Beard dropped his hands from Flynn, slowly nodding his head as he took a step back.

"Then she will die here. And I will not let you kill her because of your own selfishness. You have until the king is dead. Once I have made fair on my end of the deal, I am taking Emily back. With or without your help."

"Then I will go back with her."

Blood Beard laughed. "There is no room for pirates where we come from. You will only make her life harder."

THE PENNY DROPS

Emily

Lies always have a way of finding the surface. No matter how deep you bury them, like a tree, they will take root and force their way above ground. But how you care for the tree after it surfaces will determine if it will bare any fruit, or if it will rot the ground it grows in.

Emily was already stationed in a private sleeping quarter that her father had assigned to her. The bed was large enough to fit three people in, or her and one very large pirate. Tonight, they would spend the night together. Somehow, this night felt different.

But what kind of relationship is it? Are we friends? Partners?...Lovers?

She sat down at the edge of the bed and let herself fall backwards atop the comforter, leaving her legs to hang off the side.

Emily bit her lip lightly. They touched one another without a second thought, he kissed her as if he wanted to capture the very breath from her lungs. This was not something that happened between friends. And yet lovers didn't exactly describe their relationship either. Lovers build their relationship on trust and time. What Emily and Flynn had was more akin to a fleeting moment of passion.

A spark in an otherwise dark cave.

What would they label themselves as?

The door opened and Emily turned her head towards the entrance to see Flynn. Her lips curled up in a smile and she sat up on her elbows to watch him as he made his way into the room. But her smile slowly faded as she took in his appearance.

His shoulders were stiff and his expression was hard upon his face. He looked up at her and her stomach felt as though it were falling.

"How did it go?" she asked. Emily sat up from the bed to fully stand on her feet. She only needed to walk a few steps to be able to stand directly in front of him. Flynn avoided her eyes and made no attempt to reach for her. "Flynn? What happened?" she asked softly.

Emily brought her hand up and hovered over his chest, but when he had no reaction, she tried to slowly drop her arm. As soon as she began to give him space, Flynn's hand shot out and snatched her wrist, pulling her close and placing her hand over his chest. She could feel the rapid beating of his heart through his shirt.

"Flynn, you're scaring me," Emily gasped. He finally met her gaze and something in his eyes seemed distant.

"Please, Princess. I have tried to be patient," he began. His voice was pleading, yet demanding at the same time. "I wanted to wait until you were ready. But I need you to tell me the truth about who you are. Even if it makes me a selfish man."

Emily tried to swallow down the lump in her throat. "W-what did my Father tell you?"

Flynn shook his head, his voice turning solemn and rough.

"Nothing. He said it is not his truth to tell. So, *please.*" Flynn kept his hand covering hers, holding it tight against his chest. "Tell me who you are. I have to know everything if I am to be able to protect you. I need the truth, Emily. No more lies. No more running away."

Emily peered up at Flynn's eyes and rather than anger at her deceptions, he looked pained. His other hand brushed her hair behind her ear, and that's when she saw it. He looked as though he had failed at something.

She dropped his gaze to look at her hand pressed over his heart. In this moment, she might break it, but she *would* break it if she kept lying to him. And her heart, her heart felt as though it was on the brink of collapse.

She took a deep breath and met his gaze again.

"Yes," she nodded her head once. "The full truth..." The words seemed caught in her throat.

"Please, Princess. I promise there is nothing you can say that will make me turn away from you. You have my heart—"

"No, Flynn."

He tilted his head to the side slightly as his brows knit together. "No?"

"This is what I've been hiding. What I have been struggling to find a way to tell you. We cannot be together. We cannot be together because you, this," she said, gesturing to the room around them, "*none* of this is real. I am not a princess or a psychic. I am...a girl from nowhere. I am *nobody.*"

"What do you mean this is not real?"

Emily expelled a deep breath and steeled her voice. "I am from London, England. And that night I met you, I had been reading a book called 'The Adventures of The Cross Bone Pirate Thief'. It is the story of a pirate who witnessed the brutal murder of his father, and spent all his life tracking down and plotting to kill the king with a band of his most trusted friends—"

"No...that's not possible, Emily. I am real. *This*—" he grabbed the back of her head and pulled her closer to be only a breath away from him, "—is real."

"And then he uses the masks to blend into the crowd and kill the king. The end. That is *your* story."

"Emily," he warned.

Tears welled in her eyes. She ran her tongue over her lips. "That compass you carry, there is more to the story, right? Your father didn't just give it to you. You didn't just happen to have it that day that he died. You stole it. It is why he left the port so late. Why he was pushed behind schedule. Why his route crossed paths with the Emerald Guards. You have never forgiven yourself because in the back of your mind you have always thought that if he had left on time, he wouldn't have been caught."

"Emily—"

"And-and—" she pressed on through her tears, "I was supposed to leave once you killed the king. The story would be over and I would leave, but it hurts so much—" Emily choked on a cry as tears slid down her cheeks, only to be wiped away by the pad of Flynn's thumb. His worried expression turned even more pained as he stared down at her. "I-I wanted to tell you, but I thought you w-wouldn't believe me! And what was the point if I was always going to leave you anyway—"

"Hush, Princess." He pulled her against his chest. "That

night," he began, pulling back enough to look down at her. "I was certain I saw a glowing light on the streets. And when I tried to get a better look, that is when I saw you." He caressed the back of her head with his hand until her breaths began to even out. "I have to say, having my history dissected like that is not easy to hear. And, I still might need some time, but I do not believe you are spinning falsehoods right now."

Emily pulled away from his chest to look up at him. "Are you sure? Do you really believe me?"

"I have to. I mean, you've always seemed to know what my next steps would be. I am sure impossible things have happened before." Flynn hesitated. "Still, thinking that all the suffering in this world, was knowingly created for entertainment, that seems like a cruelty I can't understand."

The guilt, to her shock, manifested into something much deeper. It morphed into shame. She enjoyed his book. She enjoyed reading it for her entertainment, but it was not just suffering in his story.

"Hope," she finally whispered. Flynn's brows furrowed as he looked down at her. "Your world was not only suffering. You taught others to have hope in the face of evil, and to never back down from doing what's right. A lesson I should have paid more attention to, I must admit."

He let out a quick breath as he nodded his head. "Then, we have to finish the story. But there is one thing you got wrong. Us."

She looked up at him quizzically.

He gave her a gentle smile that didn't reach his eyes as he walked her backwards. The back of her knees hit the bed causing her to sit down on the edge. Flynn lowered himself to the ground until he was kneeling, while still holding her hands. His hardened expression softened as his eyes met hers.

"This is not nothing." His deep voice rang with finality. "If it is as you say, and we are in a book, then that makes you the most real thing I have ever known."

"But you cannot love me, Flynn. That is not your story—"

"Then rewrite the story, Emily. So that I may spend the rest of my days getting to know the real you."

"What if you change your mind about me?" she whispered. "I might not have another chance at going home."

"In all the chaos and change that has haunted this life of mine, you are the one thing that has become a constant. Stay with me, Emily. Promise me that you will not disappear to your world."

Emily's eyes watered again as she slowly nodded her head.

"Yes," she whispered. "I want to stay." Her admission should have shocked her, but it didn't. She felt...happy.

Flynn held her gaze until her tears slowly stopped falling. He leaned in and pressed a possessive kiss upon her lips as she pulled her hands from his and wrapped them around his neck. His tongue caressed her lip and she opened her mouth for him. Flynn ran his rough hands under her dress and up her legs until he was squeezing both of her thighs.

"*Fuck*," he muttered.

Without warning, Flynn pulled her hips flush against his waist, forcing her legs around him and causing her dress to bunch around her waist as he stood. He crawled onto the bed and laid her down, resting her head on the pillows.

"Emily," Flynn growled as he pushed her dress back, exposing her sex. As Flynn knelt in front of her, she got a glimpse of his hardened cock. But, before she could take him in, Flynn grabbed her by the wrists and forced her hands above her head.

"I dare," Flynn started, grinding himself against her exposed core, "any man to tell me that what I feel for you is not real." Emily let out a low moan as his hardened cock, still covered by his pants, ground against her once more. The rough fabric rubbing against her clit. In a quick movement, Flynn pulled her hand to his hardened length and continued. "The way you make me feel is not just a story. *This* is real. The way I have wanted to claim you as mine is real, and I will kill any man who tries to tell me otherwise with no remorse."

"Flynn," Emily gasped, running her palm over him — making him groan. Emily looked up at Flynn, meeting his lust-filled eyes as she started to slowly stroke him through his pants.

"Fuck, Emily," Flynn groaned, letting her other hand undo his belt. "I meant what I said. There is nothing you can tell me that will make me turn my back on you. Even if you told me you wanted nothing to do with me one day..." Flynn let out a low laugh as he pulled his pants down to expose his dark hair that trailed down the sharp V-line of his abdomen. "I might just kidnap you again because, Emily, I am not a good man...so I am asking you now. Do you want this? Even knowing the kind of man I am?"

She nodded her head rapidly, pushing her hips forward so her pussy could grind against his cock.

"Please, Flynn," she begged.

Flynn growled, hastily pushing her legs apart and lowering his lips to trail kisses down her legs and towards the apex of her thighs.

"Flynn," Emily cried, becoming impatient with his tenderness. Before Emily could say another word, the roughness of Flynn's tongue was running over her clit. Without realizing how much she needed to feel Flynn, Emily let out a cry of pleasure.

"Sing for me, Princess," Flynn said between strokes of his tongue. "Let every dastardly pirate on this ship know that you are mine."

Emily knew that she should at least try to hide the sounds of her pleasure from everyone above deck. But, as the tip of Flynn's tongue circled her sensitive clit, and moved down to her entrance, she couldn't force herself to care. Without warning, Flynn's tongue thrust into her, causing her back to arch.

"Stay still," Flynn ordered as he pushed her down by her waist, bringing the pad of his thumb to tend to her clit.

"Oh god," Emily moaned as she weaved her fingers into his hair, pulling him closer as she ground herself against his face. Flynn's tongue continued to ruthlessly fuck her, but before she could find release the pirate pulled away. Before Emily could protest, he thrust two fingers into her.

"You are soaked for me," Flynn mused, his lips trailing up her body. Emily kept her legs pushed open, making sure as not to hinder Flynn's movements. Emily's head sank into the pillows as Flynn's lips nipped at her throat. Without pulling away from her, Flynn used his free hand to pull a hidden knife from his belt. She gasped as he used the serrated edge to trace up the fabric of her corset. He carefully ran the blade up the center, cutting string after string, slowly exposing her fully to him. "I will not be denied access to all of you, Emily."

Her breath hitched as the final string snapped, causing the corset to fall from her body as Flynn tossed the blade to the floor and lowered his head to kiss and bite across her left breast.

"Flynn, I-I need you now," Emily practically yelled, his fingers pulling out of her.

"As you wish," Flynn said against her neck, his breath grazing her nipple. His voice was dark, a promise of what was to come. Emily brought her hands back to his head, raking her nails against his scalp as he lined himself up with her entrance.

"Princess," Flynn whispered, smirking as he leaned over her.

"Pirate," Emily pleaded, the head of his cock nudging her entrance.

"Tell me you are mine."

Flynn's order was final. If Emily wanted him to continue she would have to say the words he wanted, and she did not care. She would say the words a hundred times over if it meant she could stay with him. If it meant that she could be his.

"I-I am you-"

Before she could finish her words, Flynn thrust himself into her until he was at the base. His invasion sent sparks throughout her body. Ecstasy coursed through her as he began to pump in and out of her, leaving no space to exist between them. And oh—*oh*—she was going to give all of herself to him.

"Princess," he grunted as he stilled his movements, holding his rigid form utterly still above her. She looked up at him with tear-filled eyes only to see a fiendish smirk plastered across his face. "I think," he started, only moving forward just enough to offer the slightest bit of relief, but not enough to push her any closer to that edge she so eagerly wished for. "That you should still be punished for lying to me, Emily."

"No, not now," she pleaded. She pushed her hips

forward, but in an instant, he held both of her hands in one of his, freeing his other hand to have a firm grip on her waist, stopping her from seeking any pleasure from him.

"Remember, Emily, if a princess wishes to be rewarded, she must first be a good girl."

His words did more than send a heat rippling to her core. She felt determined, challenged even, to win his approval. For him to tell her what a good job she has done pleasing him.

Emily looked up at Flynn through her teary eyes and her long lashes. "Please, Captain, let me show you how sorry I am...let me please you," she whispered.

He muttered a curse under his breath, and then there it was. That rough pleasure tinged with pain that she so desperately needed. He thrust forward, pushing himself deeper within her. A gasp tore from her throat as he pulled out and slammed back in again.

"Show me, Emily," he commanded, his voice straining against his own pleasure. "How good you can be. Tell me how real I feel."

"Yes!" she screamed as she met him thrust for thrust. She impaled herself on his cock as he thrust harder, faster, wilder. And she met each one with a desperation that she had never known before. "More!" she begged as she inched closer to the promised release.

"Fuck, Princess," he growled as he gave one more ravenous thrust and instantly, she toppled over that glorious edge. She let out a choked cry as he dropped her hands only to use both of his to hold her painfully tight against him, pushing his shaft as deep as he could go. Both of their bodies tensed and shook as their combined releases took over.

He held her in place for another moment. Sweat beaded

his forehead and dripped down his temple as he panted over top of her. He dropped her hips, but made no attempt to pull away from her. She watched him with dazed eyes as he sat back on his knees—still inside of her—so he could pull off his sweat dampened shirt, revealing the solid contours of his muscled form. Flynn tossed the shirt to the side.

When he looked back down at her, the dark strands of his hair had begun to fall out of their hold, and hung at either sides of his face. As his eyes met hers, she felt the sensation of something *growing* inside of her, filling her, stretching her, and as her eyes widened, he only smirked.

"What, Princess? Did you think one round of your pleasure would be enough to sate me?"

A MASK AND A MASQUERADE

Flynn

Heaven does not deserve its name, for nothing could ever compare itself to the divinity that was becoming one with her.

Emily rested her head on his chest as she ran her hands up and down his abdomen. The soft press of her nails against his skin sent slight shivers through his body. His arm wrapped around her, holding her exactly where she belonged—beside him.

"So, he said he would help you?" Emily asked as she angled her head to look up at Flynn.

He nodded his head as he ran his fingers in circles on her shoulder. "Yes, he will offer his armada and his men, and go along with our plan. Though, he was very clear about wanting to keep you safe..." Flynn's voice trailed off as he looked down at her.

"Did he say anything else?"

Flynn hesitated. "No, he just worries for you."

Emily hummed in agreement. "I worry for him, too. He

has been trapped here for so long. Alone. I cannot imagine what he has been through."

Trapped.

That word rung through Flynn's mind.

"Do you feel trapped here?" he asked.

Emily shook her head against Flynn's chest. "No. I mean, at first, yes. But I don't think trapped is a word I would use anymore. I feel freed. Back home, I could never try to go on such an adventure."

"Tell me more. About your world, about your family."

"My world," she started, taking a moment before she continued, "is not much different than yours, I suppose. However, women do not possess the same rights as men. We cannot work, or go to school, or speak out of turn without punishment. We can not have our own money or...own a house."

"That sounds dreadful," he muttered, pulling her closer against him.

"It's not all bad," she said. "There are things I miss."

"Like?"

"There are always new inventions. Like just recently, I saw a typewriter for the very first time. It was incredible." She looked up to him and once she saw his face, she laughed softly before laying her head back down on his chest. "It is an invention that allows one to write. However, instead of using ink and a quill, you only need to press the letters with your fingers. The typewriter will do the rest."

Flynn laughed. "Sounds like sorcery."

"I also miss my mother..." Her voice turned plaintive. "She is probably worried sick. She lost my father without an answer years ago, and I have been gone for so long now. She's probably banging down the door of the bobbies, or, guards," she corrected, "trying to find me." Her voice drifted off. She continued to draw lines across Flynn's chest.

"She sounds like she loves you very much."

"She is strict, but all of it is only out of love. She doesn't want me to struggle. Though, I think that she forgets about my happiness at times. She is consumed with giving me a good life, so that I will not struggle as she has." Emily shrugged her shoulders against Flynn. "I also want the chance to make my own mistakes, and have my own struggles, and with that, find my own adventures."

"You will," he assured. "When will you tell your father?"

Emily stayed silent for a moment then sighed. "After the masquerade ball. I will help send him home. And then..."

"And then?"

She looked up at him and smiled. "Then we will see where *our* story takes us. Besides, I always thought you needed a second book."

"I like the sound of that, Princess."

As they lay in bed, they let the calm before their own storm wash over them, embracing each other in the warmth that the momentary peace brought.

FLYNN WATCHED as Emily finished putting on a floor length, blood-red gown with slits going down both legs, slightly exposing her silk white skin when she moved. She faced away from him as her hands struggled with the final ties on the back of her corset.

Tonight, Flynn would finally put an end to the Emerald King's reign. He would finally avenge his father. He would save his people and many more. He would do many things, but losing Emily would not be one of them.

He walked across the room and gently patted her hands away from the laces.

"Are you ready, Princess?" he asked as he gently spun the long ends of the string around his hands before pulling back. Emily gave a slight intake of breath before relaxing. He gathered the laces and tied them together in a series of delicate bows down the center.

"You keep asking me that," she said. She turned around and faced him after he finished tying the last knot. "Tonight will go just as we have planned."

The door slowly creaked open and both Flynn and Emily turned their heads to see Lucas and Levi, both dressed in identical black suits.

"Show time," Levi said. His usual smirk was gone, and his voice was firm.

"We will dock in a few minutes; once we do, we will not be able to communicate until we have captured the king. So," Lucas looked up beside him at Levi, "don't do anything stupid."

"Aw," Levi cooed as he leaned down to tease Lucas. "Are you worried about me?"

"Alright," Emily said, calling the attention of Flynn and the two arguing pirates to her. "We have a king to kill, so let's not waste any time. Don't you know it's impolite to keep a king waiting?"

"Aye," Flynn agreed with a smirk. "Let's put an end to this."

The group all left the room one by one, and made their way to the deck above them. Once there, Flynn looked out into the distant sea where he could make out at least twenty more ships baring the same flags as her father's. Blood Beard's army slowly closed in on the same island they were currently docking at, like a black cloud signalling impending doom.

When he looked back at Emily, she was already across the deck. Levi had just handed her the golden raven mask that she was to wear. She slipped it on and secured it behind her head, lifting her long auburn hair out from underneath.

A hand grabbing his shoulder brought his attention away from Emily. He turned to see her father staring grimly at him.

"You bring my daughter back to me, Pirate."

Flynn nodded his head. "I will keep her safe, but I cannot just let her go home. She is happy here. With me."

"She can find happiness with another. I am begging you, Flynn, do the right thing. For her sake, not for mine."

"Flynn!" Emily called out to him.

Flynn dropped her father's glare without answering him, but that did not make the older man's words dissipate from his mind.

Flynn plastered on a fake smile, hoping it was convincing as Emily approached with his mask in hand. He could see the greens of her eyes poking through the disguise and the pink of her bottom lip peaking out from the bottom of the mask.

Blood Beard brushed past Flynn to steal a final hug from Emily. They embraced for a moment before he finally released her and took a few steps back.

"I will be watching the palace from this ship. If there are any problems, if anything goes sideways, you run outside and you don't stop running until my men find you. Do you understand?"

"Father, I will be—"

"No. Emily, I only just found you. I need to know that you understand."

She released a breath and nodded her head. "Yes, Father. I understand, but there will be no need. Flynn will keep me protected."

"And what happens when he fails?" Blood Beard muttered under his breath only loud enough for Flynn to hear.

Flynn's jaw tightened as he took the wolf mask from Emily and placed it on his face. The mask covered half of his face, revealing his lower face. Once secured, he lowered his head in a small bow while offering his open hand to Emily.

"Will you do me the honor of accompanying me to the ball this evening?"

Emily laughed as she placed her hand in his. Flynn looked up to see her smile only partially blocked by the golden mask. Behind her, Levi donned a gold fox mask and Lucas wore a golden hare mask.

Emily curtsied. "It's such a thrill to be a guest of the esteemed Isaac Bensworth."

CHECK

Emily

Emily walked arm in arm with Flynn up the steps to the palace. The whole island swarmed with what she could only assume were the aristocrats of this world. Men in tightly fit suits wore masks of varying animals and colors, each one with a woman on their arm to show off like a shiny new toy.

Honestly, our worlds are so incredibly similar.

Emily let her eyes scan the crowd. In the distance, she could see Levi and Lucas entering the building with the other waitstaff who donned masks of a similar theme. On the opposite side of the palace, she could just make out her father's ships, barely visible through the trees. Night was already setting in, so the promised shroud of darkness was a blessing.

Flynn kept a hold on her arm as they reached the top of the steps.

"Do not leave my side, Princess," he whispered just loud enough for only her to hear. She looked up at him through the holes in her mask and could see his worried smile peaking out beneath his own disguise.

Emily nodded her head as they took the final steps to the guards posted at the front doors.

They looked Flynn up and down, holding their gaze on him for a few moments longer than what she was comfortable with. Her heart picked up pace and began beating against her chest while the guards remained silent.

Finally, the guard on the right spoke. "Invitations."

"Of course," Flynn responded. He opened his suit jacket and pulled out an emerald invitation with a golden crest on the front that looked like a snake. "Here you are," Flynn said as he handed the invitation over.

The guard opened it up and read whatever was written inside. His eyes darted between the invitation and Flynn before he closed it again and stepped to the side, extending his arms towards the doors.

"Please enjoy the festivities in the king's honor, Lord Bensworth."

"Next time be faster," Emily muttered as they walked past the guards. Neither of the guards lifted their heads at her snip, but out of the corner of her eye she could tell that Flynn caught her comment from the smirk showing beneath his mask.

The doors opened and revealed a white palace decorated with golden serpents mounted on the walls. Emily looked closer and noticed their eyes were made of emerald. A large chandelier hung high above them with flickering candles lighting the ballroom. Soft music filled the room as bodies swayed among each other.

Flynn leaned down to whisper in her ear as they entered the room, his breath dancing across her skin. "Enjoying this?"

"Well, you're the one who wanted me to be royalty. Can I not be a little demanding?"

"Be as demanding as you wish, Princess. Your wish is my command," he cooed.

As they walked further into the ballroom, the music grew louder. She could make out the distinct sound of a cello, a harp, and a few violins.

Flynn led her by hand into the dozens of dancing pairs. Everyone was dressed in bright colors ranging from emerald to white, so Flynn and Emily were already sticking out.

Flynn pulled her close as he wrapped his hand around her waist. Emily wrapped one arm around his neck while the other hand held his out to the side. They swayed and moved about the room, giving both of them a chance to survey the area around them. Emily could make out the hare mask Lucas was wearing, seeing he remained stationed at the back of the room. When his eyes met hers, he nodded.

"Lucas is ready, but I do not see Levi," she whispered to Flynn.

"He has most likely already made it to the second floor, and it seems as though our guest of honor has just arrived."

Flynn suddenly dipped Emily while keeping his hand firmly on her waist. Her head fell back as Flynn ran his hand up the slit in her dress, pulling her thigh against his waist.

Emily looked towards the entrance to see a tall older man with a mask only covering his eyes. In the center of the mask was a brown cobra.

Flynn pulled Emily back up slowly, holding her inner thigh close against his hip for a moment longer than what was necessary.

"That's him?" she whispered.

He leaned down to whisper in her ear, no doubt getting

a better look at the king. "Yes, and it seems as though you have caught his attention."

Emily tried to turn her head, but Flynn caught her chin and shifted her mask to the side just enough to steal a kiss. She instantly melted into his touch and she began to lose herself.

The sound of a man clearing his throat had Flynn pulling away from her, letting her mask fall back in place. When she opened her eyes, Flynn seemed like an entirely different person. He smiled from ear to ear and swayed slightly.

"Ah!" he exclaimed as he stepped back from Emily and gave a sloppy bow. "Your Majesty! Thank you for hosting such an incredible party. Truly, this will be a night to remember."

Emily looked up at the king. She noticed he was even more gluttonous looking than he was described in the book. Every wrinkled finger was adorned with diamonds and jewels, his outfit looked to be spun with golden thread, and his eyes unapologetically roamed her body. There was an unmistakable and unhidden covetousness in his leer that made a cold shiver run down her spine.

This was a look she knew.

He looked at her like she was a trophy, a stepping stool to gain bragging rights.

"And, Sweet Raven, what do you think of this event?" the king asked.

Emily bowed her head as she curtsied. She slowly lifted her gaze to meet his as she stood up again. "Emily, Your Majesty," she responded. "It is beyond words. Truly, something to see."

He snatched her hand and out of the corner of her eye

Emily could see Flynn tense. The king placed a wet, slow kiss on the top of her hand.

Disgusting.

"Well, it seems like your date has indulged too much in the refreshments. Why don't you join me so that you may enjoy tonight to your fullest?"

Flynn took a wobbly step forward. "I apologize, but we must decline—"

"I insist," Emily interrupted. She glanced back at Flynn and his smile didn't fade, but she could tell from the lines on his neck and the stiffness in his form that he was anything but alright. She looked back at the king and offered a soft smile. "I would be honored to entertain you."

His eyes widened as he once again let his gaze roam over her body.

"We can hopefully entertain each other," he said in a mock of a sensual tone that made her skin crawl. "The pleasure of such a beautiful raven is of the upmost importance."

Emily walked forward, not chancing another look at Flynn.

This is an opportunity. I know his kind. He is the worst part of every man back home. He does not think someone like me could pose a threat. To someone like him, I am nothing but someone new to dominate.

A new pet to add to his collection.

The king wrapped his spindly, ring-covered hand around her waist as he led her to the other end of the ballroom. Once people noticed the king, they all began to slowly part ways for him.

The king stopped and pulled Emily close so that their bodies were pressed against one another. They began to sway slowly to the music, but Emily could hardly hear it anymore over the sound of her own beating heart.

"So tell me," the king whispered. "How come I have never seen you at one of my events before? Surely I never would have missed such a beautiful guest."

"Oh well, I don't get out much. Lord Bensworth just happened to catch my attention, but you," she said, holding his gaze, "you have captivated me. It's an honor to be in your presence tonight."

The king smiled as he spun them around, giving Emily and opportunity to see Flynn keeping his eyes firm upon her.

"The honor is mine. However," he began, stealing her attention away from Flynn, "I do find these events to get quite crowded, don't you?"

"Are you a psychic?" she mused. "You read my mind. How about a private tour?"

The king gave a perverted smile as he began to leave the ballroom, keeping a firm hold on her waist. Two Emerald Guards moved to follow them but the king dismissed them with a wave of his hand. "I believe a lady should appreciate some privacy. Give us a moment and busy yourselves."

The guards gave a quick bow in response and turned on their heals in unison, heading back towards the main ballroom.

Once they left, the king once again began walking forward, pulling Emily along. She nearly tripped over her own feet at his sudden excitement. The king quickly led her out of sight of the rest of his guests, down a darkened hallway that seemed to go on forever. The walls were decorated with paintings of himself with different women. Each one looking younger and younger the deeper they ventured.

"Shall we start with the bedroom?"

"How about your office? I like seeing a man at work."

The king laughed as he nodded his head. "I like a woman who knows what she wants."

Emily forced a smile as she tried to swallow the rising sickness she felt in the pit of her stomach.

Please be in the office, Levi.

Emily looked over her shoulder and a wave of ease washed over her as she saw Flynn quietly trailing behind them.

The king quickened his pace and, at first she did not know why, until they stopped outside of a large set of arching wooden doors. The king pulled them open and pushed Emily inside, almost causing her to trip as he slammed the door shut behind himself.

"Now," the king said. "Shall we let the entertainment begin?"

"How about a drink first?" Emily suggested as she walked over to his desk and leaned against it.

The king scowled as he let out a breath before turning and walking over to a tall glass cabinet. Emily let her eyes roam the office. It was modern enough. Dark wooden walls, tall paintings of himself, large arching windows and—Emily stopped as her eyes reached the curtains. They were massive and billowed down to the floor, almost completely hiding the man standing behind them—Levi. He nodded his head as if to say 'keep going.' Through his fox mask, she could see that his eyes were cold, a stark contrast to their usual warmth. Emily cleared her throat and brought her attention back to the king.

He opened up the tall cabinet and pulled out a tall dark bottle with a singular wine glass.

"You're not partaking?" she asked, keeping her voice even. Her eyes kept darting between the king and the door. Flynn was most likely on the other side, waiting.

"I would prefer to be completely sober for this, Raven." He poured the dark red liquid into the glass, filling it halfway. He handed her the wine and she mouthed a, 'thank you,' as she took it. He watched her with anticipation as she brought the glass to her mouth and took the smallest sip.

The bitterness danced across her tongue and she wanted to spit it out, but she swallowed.

"So," she began, "how does a man like you get his wealth?"

The king stalked closer to her so that he was standing just a few steps away. "You're asking me to divulge my secrets? Without so much as taking off your mask and showing me the rest of your face?"

"Don't you know? Secrets are what make seduction so thrilling. You never know who you're really with." She took another bitter sip of the wine.

"You say that and yet you wish to know my own secrets."

"You tell me yours and I'll show you mine."

The kings heated gaze felt like acid on her skin. His tongue darted out to wet his lips. "Well, my coin is made in many ways I suppose. Trading being the biggest one."

Her stomach flipped. "And what exactly do you trade? Weapons, materials...or something less than above the bar?"

His eyes darkened. "What exactly are you insinuating, Raven? Am I not the king? Do I not own these lands? Do I not own my subjects? As far as I am concerned, everything has a price. Everything is fair trade."

Emily felt herself grow bold. Maybe it was the anger at the injustice or, perhaps it was the fact that she knew three pirates with a vendetta would protect her. "You believe they are to be owned? They are people, not cattle."

"Well, why don't we discuss business after we discuss pleasure?" he hissed. He took a step closer and Emily shot her leg up, pressing her heel against his chest before kicking him back slightly. Even though he was older, his build was solid and he only stumbled back two steps.

"I think I am no longer interested in pleasure, Your Majesty."

His face began to redden as he advanced again, grabbing her wrist and slamming her back against the desk. The wine crashed onto the floor and the glass shattered beneath them.

"Do you think you can waste my time and make a fool out of me, girl? Besides, I think you owe me a look at that sharp tongue of yours."

Emily's gaze hardened as she looked up at the king without anymore fear.

"I would be very careful about how you treat me," she said with a coldness in her voice that surprised even her.

"Or what? You will nag me to death?" He barked a mocking laugh that echoed through the room.

"Oh, well, I am not actually the one you need to be worried about."

"And who would I, the Emerald King, need to be worried about?" he whispered.

Emily looked behind the king to see Flynn walking up behind him, pressing the barrel of his pistol against the side of the king's head.

The king froze. His eyes moved to see Flynn in his mask towering over him. Her pirate stared down at Emily with a look of possession in his eyes.

"I thought you said a sword was a gentleman's weapon?" she teased.

"Do not ask me to be a gentle man when you are in danger."

Flynn grabbed the king and ripped him off Emily,

tossing him to the floor. He kept his eyes and gun trained on the king, but still made sure to extend a hand to help Emily. She grabbed it and pulled herself upright, standing beside him. Levi was already grabbing the rope he had hidden in the room and Lucas was securing the door.

"Tie him up quick," Flynn ordered.

Levi did not hesitate in wrapping the rope around the king, pulling hard enough that his knuckles went white. He only stopped pulling when the king began to squeal like a pig.

"Now," Levi said with a rough voice. He took off his mask and within the same movement, whipped it at the king's face. The mask went flying off into the distance, ricocheting off the floor. The king doubled over and swayed slightly. Once he was able to sit back up, blood trickling down his face, Levi towered over him. "Where the fuck is my sister?"

MATE

Flynn

The king looked up at Levi, without so much of a hint of guilt. "This is about a girl?" The king barked a laugh. "Do you think I keep track of every pretty face that comes through these parts? Hm?"

Levi kicked the king in the chest, sending him flying onto his back with a loud thud.

Emily came to stand beside Flynn, she lifted her hand to her face and began to take off the mask, but Flynn shot his arm out and grabbed her wrist, halting her movements.

Her eyes flicked up to his, and he shook his head.

"Keep it on, Princess. I do not want him to see your face."

Understanding flashed across Emily's eyes and she nodded her head, dropping her hand away from the mask.

Flynn looked back to the king, who was still coughing and trying to catch his breath.

"I would answer him," he said. "He is not a patient man. Tends to be rather impulsive."

The king angled his head to look back at Flynn as he brought himself to his knees again. His eyes narrowed in disgust. "Who are you, really? Or are you really just as much of a sleazy lord as they say? Doing anything for coin?"

Flynn laughed as he grab the bottom of his mask and began to slowly lift it. "If anyone here should be judged by their motivation for coin, and their morals—or lack there of —it is not I." He dropped the mask to the floor as he stared down, face to face, with the man he had been hunting since his father was murdered.

The king's eyes widened and the corners of his lips twitched into a half smile. "Flynn Sawyer, leader of the army of the impoverished and forgotten. I must say, you are late to your appointment with the gallows."

"You are in no position to be making such threats, when you will most likely never see a sunrise again."

"And how do you plan to escape, Flynn Sawyer? Will you have your woman seduce the guards next or sleep with them—"

Flynn's fist connected with the king's jaw with a crack that echoed through the room. "Actually, we plan on using the front door," he spat.

The king spat out the thick blood from his mouth onto the floor as his serpentine mask fell off of his face. "Well," he hissed, "did you really think I wasn't expecting some form of attack? You and your followers have been sinking my ships left and right. And if I don't come down within the next half hour, no one is leaving this island. Then what?"

"Enough chit chat," Lucas said. The king turned back to face Lucas and Levi. "We cannot stay long. So answer him. Where is his sister?"

"Do you know how many women I have sold off? How should I know?"

"No!" Levi yelled. "None like her. You would remember her. She has one arm. She had it amputated at birth. She has golden hair, and green eyes."

"The broken one? Yes, I remember her."

"Then where. Is. She?" Levi asked again.

"Gone."

Lucas stepped forward. "What do you mean, gone?"

"Like I said, gone. She did work within these walls, hosting parties and *entertaining* guests, but I got an offer on her last month. She's been sold off—"

Levi screamed as he kicked the king in the chest again. He moved to kneel over the king as he began slamming his fists into the man's face. The sound of bones crunching and blood splattering filled the room, accompanied by moans of pain.

Lucas ran over to Levi and hugged him from behind as he began pulling him back. "We still don't have answers, Levi," he whispered to his friend.

"Fine," Levi yelled, shrugging Lucas off his back as he stood. "Who did you sell her to?"

The king's head lolled to the side as he spat out blood and began to cough. "You'll all be hanged for this. Each and every one of you."

Flynn scoffed. "Well, clearly you're not that hurt if you can still talk."

"Fuck you," the king muttered. "Should have died with your father."

Flynn took a step forward, but Emily held his arm back. He looked down at her and a pang of guilt shot through his stomach. She looked scared. Flynn pulled Emily close so his arm rested over both of her shoulders. "Be brave for a bit longer, Princess," he whispered.

Lucas spoke up. "Who did you sell her to?"

"I don't know," the king answered. "He hid his identity. Mysterious guy showed up to the island one day. Offered enough coin for me to not ask questions. But it wasn't just her he purchased. It was all of them. When I asked for his name, he only said that he was the Harbinger."

"What did he look like?" Levi asked.

Lucas looked at the door, then back at the group. "We are running out of time."

The king sighed. "What about 'hid his identity' is lost on you, boy? He wore a white tiger skull mask. With a black cloak. Whoever he is, he seems worse than me. Darker. More sinister. Why else would ya go through the troubles of hiding yourself like that?"

Levi turned and began slowly walking to the doors, every few steps he would stumble.

The king spat more blood on the floor as Lucas pulled his gun from his jacket. He loaded the pistol with one single bullet.

"So my truths have not been enough to earn my life nor your mercy?" the king asked.

Lucas shook his head. "If you answer me one thing, then I shall spare your life." He cocked the gun back and pressed the barrel against the king's forehead. "You sent men to my Father because you wanted me so bad. When he refused, they slaughtered him. So, if I was so important to you, what. Is. My. Name?"

"Please—" the gun went off with a loud bang and a puff of smoke. The king's body hit the ground with a wet thud.

Lucas lifted his gun and blew away the smoke before placing it back in his jacket. "Wrong answer."

Levi slammed the door shut, causing Flynn, Emily, and Lucas to all look towards him. "We've got trouble. Guards. More than we thought."

A cannon went off in the distance, shaking the palace slightly.

"Father," Emily whispered. She pulled away from Flynn and ran to the window, throwing it open to reveal a rope tied to the banister. Flynn caught up to her to see the king's ships intercepting their armada, and a group of soldiers closing in on her father's ship.

"Time to go," Flynn ordered. "Now!"

As if on cue, guards began to bang on the door. A quick glance over his shoulder confirmed that before Levi began running towards them, he locked it. But it wouldn't hold for long. With each impact the door received from the other side, it inched closer and closer to bursting open.

Emily stepped back from the window, looking at the rope that led to her father's ship, and then back at Flynn. "Please tell me whatever escape you have in mind does not involve throwing ourselves out of a window?"

"It does not involve throwing ourselves out a window," he said as he began tearing off two long strips of curtain. The relief on Emily's face was short lived as he handed her a piece. "It involves gliding down a rope at high speeds, onto your father's ship. But worry not, Princess, while I have no intention of letting you fall, I also have no intention of being caught today."

The guards slammed against the door again as Levi and Lucas followed suit, ripping their own thick sections off from the curtain.

Emily muttered a curse half-heartedly as she ran to the balcony. She threw her legs over so she was balancing on the edge as she tossed the cloth over the rope, wrapping each end tightly around her hands.

"Remember," Flynn whispered from a step behind her

as he watched her ready herself. "Don't let go until you reach the ship."

He watched Emily take a deep breath before he pushed her off, sending her gliding down the rope, screaming the entire way. Her body moved and swayed with the wind. He watched until she finally reached the bottom, and let go. The motion sent her body rolling, but she quickly got to her feet.

Next was Lucas.

Before he even made it halfway, Levi dropped off the balcony. The half-witted pirate slammed into Lucas, sending them both tumbling to the deck.

Flynn stepped onto the banister just as the door burst open and ten Emerald Guards came pouring into the room, swords drawn.

"Halt!" one of the guards yelled as they closed in on Flynn.

He turned his head to look over his shoulder, a smirk playing at his lips. "I must offer my condolences. I'm afraid I will be missing my appointment with the gallows in the morning. How impolite of me."

Flynn pulled his pistol out and aimed it at the rope. He let off one shot, snapping the rope in half and catching it as he jumped off the balcony. His body felt weightless as it dropped with only the rope wrapped around his hand to prevent him from falling. He flew down towards the ship. Gunfire rang out behind him, mixing with the sound of Emerald Guards yelling and cannon fire colliding with the palace.

As the ship appeared beneath him, Flynn dropped his hold on the rope and fell to the deck, rolling twice before springing to his feet.

Blood Beard left Emily's side as he rushed up to the

helm of his ship. "Hoist the sails!" he yelled. "Ready the cannons!"

Flynn raced to Emily, and pulled her into a tight embrace.

"You scared me half to death, Pirate," she scolded into his shoulder.

"Then you are still halfway full of life, Princess."

WITH LOVE, COMES LOSS

Flynn

The ships raced against the crashing waves as cannon fire continued to ring out around them. Flynn looked out at sea only to find that over half of Blood Beards armada was already gone.

"They're gaining," Emily said with a nervous voice from beside him.

He looked down at her, his brows knitting together. She was right. With over half of Blood Beard's ships at the bottom of the sea, and the other half occupied with the emerald ships, they were completely alone with the last ship headed directly towards them.

For the first time, in a very long time, Flynn felt a genuine fear deep within himself. It was not for his own life, but for *hers*.

I never should have brought her with me.

"Don't suppose there is anything in my book about this?" he asked her. She shook her head, worry marred across her face as she dropped his gaze and focused on the incoming ship.

It was too close for comfort. Rather than chase from behind, it began to move beside them, revealing enough Emerald Soldiers to out-man their own crew.

"Fuck," Flynn muttered as he took a step back.

Emily turned to follow him, but he grabbed her by the arms and stopped her.

"Flynn," she begged, "what are you doing?"

"Probably something very stupid, but if we do not get them to fall back we might all die here." Flynn dropped his hold on her as he turned on his heels and raced over to the crates of grenadoes and pulled one out of the pile. He turned back to look at Emily. "Wait here, Princess."

He turned away from her and ran over to one of the nearest masts and looked up at the many swaying ropes. Cannon fire continued to sound off, only making his worry run deeper.

If they managed to board the ship, it would be a blood bath for everyone involved. This wasn't how it was supposed to go. They were supposed to kill the king, save Levi's sister, and make a clean and quiet break. But Flynn had underestimated the loyalty of the Emerald Guard.

Flynn shoved the slow match into an open oil lamp, lighting it on fire. He held the grenadoe tight in his arm as he used the ropes to climb up the mast. His muscles strained as he raced to the top, fighting against the rocking of the ship and the raging winds of the sea. The smoke from the slow match began to fill his lungs as it burned lower and lower, inching closer to the gunpowder-filled iron ball.

As he reached the top of the mast, he opened his arm, rolling the grenadoe into his hand. He watched as the fire neared the base, he waited as the enemy ship grew closer, until the heat began to burn his hand and he could hear the vile cries of the Emerald Guard.

He pitched his arm up and launched the grenadoe, sending it flying towards the enemy ship. The moment it landed, the ship erupted in chaos as the deafening sound of the bomb going off washed over them.

Fire soon began to grow, lighting up the darkness of the sea with an eerie orange glow. He wanted to bask in it, as the flame set ablaze their ship, he wanted to enjoy the heat of the fire. But instead of warmth, his blood ran cold as he heard Emily let out a blood curling scream.

"Flynn!" she yelled.

He looked down and saw Emily, sword drawn, staring down the barrel of a gun of one of the Emerald Guards who must have swung over the ship as Flynn was distracted with the grenadoe.

Pure fear as cold as ice rushed through his blood. Blood Beard must have seen the sight as well, because he yelled out for his daughter with the kind of fear in his voice that only a parent could make.

Without a second thought, Flynn jumped off the mast, holding the rope tight as he swung down. He screamed as the Emerald Guard grew closer to Emily, causing the guard to turn his attention towards Flynn. The guard aimed his gun at Flynn. A shot rang out in the air as Flynn dropped the rope and tackled the bastard to the ground, ignoring the blaring pain throughout his body as he landed hard atop the guard.

They wrestled for the gun, each throwing punches. Flynn tuned out the screams of his girl from nowhere and the calls of her father and his crew members. The pain grew more focused as Flynn twisted the pistol around. He ripped it from the guard's grasp, cocked it back, and let off a single shot directly into the guard's head, ending the fight.

Flynn jumped to his feet as he looked behind him at Emily. The color had drained from her face as tears filled her eyes.

"Flynn!" she yelled as she dropped her sword and ran up to him. "Oh God, no—please, please no!"

He took a step forward, but winced as he looked down. He gave an empty laugh as he saw the deep red in his abdomen slowly spread across his shirt.

Flynn fell to the ground as Emily reached him, catching his head before he hit the deck. A crowd began to form around them, but neither the crowd or the burning ship made much noise. All he could focus on was her.

"Are you hurt, Emily?"

"No," she cried, pulling at his shirt trying to open it. "But you—"

He placed his hands over hers, stopping her frantic movements. "I am fine, so long as you are safe. If I wasn't fast enough, it would have been you. I am glad it was me, Princess."

The truth of his words sank in. The realization that he truly almost lost her, made his heart feel like it was being ripped apart by guilt.

It could have been her.

Flynn closed his eyes.

I cannot keep her safe here.

Finally, he truly heard Blood Beard's plea to do what was right for his daughter. If she were to stay with Flynn, as much as he wanted her by his side, she would never be safe.

He opened his eyes and saw a myriad of blue and white begin to form on the ship, behind Emily. It looked like a ball of lightening.

"Emily!" Blood Beard yelled as he pushed through the crowd, falling to his knees beside them.

"Father," she cried, "do something! Help him, please!"

"Cap!" Levi and Lucas yelled as they came to kneel on his other side.

"Medic!" Lucas screamed, assessing the damage. "I need a medic!"

Everyone's voices rang out over one another, it was hard to focus in on anything.

Exhaustion began to take over his mind as warmth spread through his body. He looked behind Emily at the lightening. It began to clear up, and show the inside of a room with green walls.

So, this is your home?

Blood Beard, as well as the rest of the crew began to look at the light.

Emily paid no attention to it. She kept kneeling beside Flynn. "I'm staying right here. We promised each other book two, right?"

Flynn nodded as Blood Beard stood and walked behind Emily.

"You let me find love where it shouldn't have existed," he began, "but you have your own stories to write, and your own adventures to go on." Flynn lifted one of his hands, wincing at the pain as he reached into his pocket and pulled out his compass, handing it to her. She hesitated as she took it. "You do not have to forgive me, but please, do not forget me."

"What?" Emily asked.

Flynn whispered a broken apology as he pulled his hands from her and used his remaining strength to push her backwards into the light.

"Flynn! No! NO! I'm staying with him!" Emily screamed

as the glowing light pulled her full force into the image of the Green Room.

"I'm sorry," he whispered. "I'm sorry."

Her father looked at Flynn and bowed his head. "Thank you," he mouthed. Flynn smiled softly as Blood Beard took a final step back, falling into the image as it collapsed into nothingness, taking Emily along with it. She disappeared before his eyes without a trace, as if she never existed in the first place.

But with her warmth gone, the pain in his body began to scream out.

"What the fuck was that?" Levi yelled, his voice finally being heard by Flynn.

"Not the most important thing right now!" Lucas screamed as he started putting pressure on the gunshot wound.

Flynn grunted. "I'll explain everything, if I make it out of this."

"Medic!" Levi pleaded. "Where the fuck is the medic?!"

Lucas' voice sounded muffled as he spoke to Flynn. "Stay with us, Cap, come on! Levi, this is a lot of blood! We need to..."

The voices of his friends slowly drowned out, as if being plunged underwater.

And with another pain filled breath, darkness consumed him.

At least she is safe.

She is safe.

I protected her.

EMILY'S GAMBIT

Emily

I did try tell you that this would not be a simple story. I warned you, dear reader, that with love comes loss. A truth we all must learn. However, I think that even the most broken of hearts, can be mended with a little bit of luck, and a breath of magic.

Emily struggled against the pull of the light as she was torn away from Flynn. As the blue light started to envelop them, she saw Levi and Lucas surround Flynn, who lay on the deck, covered in blood, unmoving.

Her stomach dropped as they fell backwards, landing hard on the ground. She scrambled to her feet to try and race back to him, but the blue light turned to smoke and disappeared, leaving her to stare blankly at the familiar bookshelves of the Green Room.

"No," she whispered. Tears fell down her cheeks as she dropped to her knees. She looked down at his golden compass in her hands. A few tears fell on top of it, making it shine in the light of the Green Room. She brought the compass to her heart and hugged it tight against her chest, closing her eyes, wishing, *begging*, for some way to go back to him. "It's my fault...he wasn't supposed to die. That's not his story. He is alive, I know it. I just know it. Death cannot come for him yet. If we go back now, there could still be time—"

"Emily," her father said from behind her. He placed a hand on her shoulder, but she pulled away from his touch, standing up as she whipped her head around to look at him. His eyes widened as he stared down at her. His mouth opened and closed as if searching for words, but he said nothing except a whispered, meaningless, "I'm sorry..."

Emily shook her head. "It's fine. After all, we can be a family now. Just like *you* wanted." She tried to hide the hurt in her voice but she couldn't.

"You never would have been safe there. You never could be happy away from—"

"Happy?" Emily scoffed, her voice filling with an empty humor. "You have been gone for *years*. What do you know of what will make me happy? No, this was about you coming home. This is what *you* wanted. Not me."

Her father stared down at her, his eyes falling slightly. "And what about your mother?"

Emily looked back down at the compass in her hands, running her thumb over the engravings. "If mother had you, she would be fine."

Her father carefully placed his hand on her shoulder again. This time she made no attempt to pull away. "No parent is well, in mind or body, if they spend each night not knowing if their child is safe."

The door to the Green Room burst open causing both Emily and her father to look up at Ms. Lewis as she came barging into the room. They all froze, staring at one another.

Ms. Lewis looked between Emily and her father before finally taking in what was before her.

"Emily! Thank heavens you are alive!" she finally yelled. Her hands waved around as she hurried over to Emily, pulling her into a tight—nearly crushing—embrace. Ms. Lewis pulled away from Emily as her shocked expression hardened. "Where have you been? You have been gone for weeks! Your mother has been worried sick. Sick as a dog I tell you." She paused as she looked down at Emily's red dress from the masquerade ball. "And what on earth are you wearing?"

Emily smiled as she pulled Ms. Lewis into another embrace. "I missed you so much, and I have quite the story to tell you."

Ms. Lewis must have noticed Emily's father. Once they pulled apart, Ms. Lewis couldn't stop herself from staring. Nor could she stop her nose from crinkling and her brows from knitting together as she stared at the strange man.

"And who is this? Why is he dressed like a madman?"

Her father extended his hand, to which Ms. Lewis cautiously returned the favor, shaking it. "We haven't had the pleasure of meeting. I am Emily's father. And like she said, it is quite the story to tell. But before anything else, I would like to see my wife."

Ms. Lewis paled even further as she slowly nodded her head. "Right then...Mr. Underwood that would make you." Ms. Lewis left Emily's side as she slowly walked over to the door, holding it open. "Go home. Both of you."

Emily nodded her head as her and her father made their way out of the Green Room. Her father went first, bowing slightly to Ms. Lewis. As Emily tried to follow, Ms. Lewis grabbed Emily's arm, stilling her movements. She looked down at her librarian and smiled gently.

"Are you well?" Ms. Lewis asked.

Emily's smile fell. "I...I don't know. I met someone. But they are gone now. I couldn't help him and now he is gone. Like he never existed except for between the pages of a book."

"You are strong. You always have been. But if it's happily ever after that you want, all you must do is ask for a second chance. We all deserve one."

"I don't think it's that simple."

"Funny thing about most of our problems, if you have a bit of imagination, most things really do become that simple."

Emily smiled softly. She leaned down and kissed Ms. Lewis on the cheek. "Thank you," she whispered.

Her father yelled for her and Ms. Lewis dropped her arm as Emily pulled away.

She walked through the library that she had disappeared from weeks ago. It all seemed so different. What she once thought of as impossible adventures, she now thought of as almost...boring. After experiencing life with Flynn, nothing seemed comparable anymore.

She joined her father at the end of the library. The small bell above the door jingled as they pulled the it open, and began their walk home. It wasn't nearly as peaceful as her normal walks to the library. They were both still wearing clothes from the book. Not a single person walked by without stopping to stare at least once.

"London hasn't changed much," her father sighed as they walked by a group of older women staring and whispering among one another.

"Neither has our home. Mother kept most of your things just as you left them. She never stopped hoping that you would find your way home."

Her father hummed. "It was because of you that I could finally come back to her."

She always knew that her parents loved each other deeply. They were like swans. They only saw each other, no matter what.

The walk continued until they finally reached the front door to their house. She never really paid mind to how grand their home was. Emily found herself thinking back to Martha's small inn and how comfortable it was.

"Wait here," Emily said. "She will be shocked enough to see me. I will talk to her first."

He nodded his head as he stood against the door frame. "I've waited years for this. I can wait a few more seconds."

Emily released a breath as she grabbed the door handle and turned it. She opened the door and walked inside. The hallway was dark and the house was quiet. She closed the door with a soft click.

"Hello?" her mother called out from the living room. Her voice grew louder as she made her way to the hallway. She rounded the corner and Emily almost didn't recognize her. Her hair was disheveled and her clothes looked slept in. Her face was bare and under her eyes were purple. She looked up from the ground as she spoke, "I already made it clear I do not want any visitors right now—"

"Not even one?" Emily asked softly. Her mother froze and tears began to well in her eyes. "Mother, I am—" the wind was almost knocked out of her as her mother ran to her and hugged her.

"*Home*," she said, smiling as tears ran down her face. "You're home. Thank you, thank you for bringing my baby home." Her mother continued to whisper into Emily's shoulder, "I thought I lost you. Just like your father."

"Mother, actually, there is something I need to tell you."

"No," her mother said, pulling away from Emily. "There is something I need to tell *you*. I never should have pushed you for something you didn't want. This whole time you were gone I kept wondering why. But then I realized it too late. You already told me what you want and I ignored you. You want more than what you can find here. I don't know if what you are choosing is the right choice. However, I will be there to support you. I will let you make your own mistakes. The house is taken care of so we can go. Wherever you want, whatever you want to see."

Emily felt her eyes begin to water all over again. She cleared her throat and blinked away the tears. "Well, about that...I found someone while I was gone..."

"What do you mean?" her mother asked.

The door slowly opened and Emily stepped to the side so that her mother could see him. He walked into the doorway and slowly raised his head to look at her.

"It's a little late, but I'm home, my love."

Her mother stood still, shaking her head as more tears fell past her cheeks. "A-Angus...You're," she began as he took another careful step towards her. "You're so old," she said, smiling as she cried. He cupped her face and wiped away the tears with his thumbs.

"Aye," he whispered. "And you're as beautiful as the day I met you. I'm sorry it took so long to come back to you."

"All these years," she began in a slow, broken voice. "All these years!" she yelled this time. She took a step forward and slapped her hands over his chest, her hurt and anger was written across her face as she looked at him. But as he looked at her, he looked happy. "I refused to believe it, but in the back of my mind I thought you were dead," she admitted through tears.

He placed his hands over top of hers, stilling her movements. "I am so sorry, my love," he said softly. "I was a fool for seeking adventure away from you, when you were all the adventure I ever needed. I will never let myself forget that again. I only ask for a second chance with you."

Her mother shook her head before looking up at him. "You're a fool for thinking you need to ask. You're here now," she said, glancing between him and Emily. "But how? What happened? And how did Emily find you?"

"That's a long story," Emily said, walking up to her parents.

"And a rather remarkable one at that," her father added.

Her mother's voice firmed. "If you think I am letting either of you out of my sight anytime soon, you've got another thing coming. I will put on some tea, and you will tell me everything. No one is sleeping tonight."

THEY SPENT many hours into the night explaining what happened. First, her father explained the storm, the bright light, and waking up inside the book. He explained how it took him a while to understand what happened, but no matter what he did, he couldn't find a way home. Then Emily told her mother about the library, the storm, and waking up in Oakden where she met Flynn. Although, she left out the kidnapping and a few *other things*. She told her mother about how she figured out how to get home and when she found her father in Butchers Harbor.

They went through a few pots of tea, only stopping the stories to put a new one on. By the time they finished, the sun had already risen. But the entire time, her mother never once grew tired or stopped listening.

"And then what happened?" her mother asked, taking

another sip of tea that had likely gone cold. Her father was seated beside her mother, his arm wrapped tightly around her. He had changed into his old clothes halfway through the night.

"And then...we left."

"What?" she asked, setting down the cup of tea. "So, what happened to Flynn?"

"I...I don't know."

Her mother's lips tightened into a thin line as she looked at Angus, and then back at Emily. "He sounds like a wonderful man."

Emily smiled fondly, looking off into the distance. "He is. He is kind and funny and passionate for what he believed in. He wanted to help his people."

Her parents looked at one another. Her father nodded and her mother smiled.

"Well," her mother began, "it sounds like he still has a lot of work to do. He could probably use some help."

Emily's eyebrows furrowed. "What are you saying?"

"Your whole life I have tried to stop you from doing anything dangerous. I thought I was protecting you but really, I was protecting myself. I think it's about time we all get a little adventure."

"Together," her father added.

Emily's heart began to race as the feeling of hope began to fill her chest. "But you said you wanted to come home, Father. It is all you have wanted to do."

"London isn't what I wanted. It's this right here. My family is my home. And besides," he continued, "your mother is right. I too hurt you in my own efforts to protect you."

Emily shook her head. "How would we even get back in?"

Her father shrugged his shoulders. "We got in twice and as the saying goes, the third time's the charm."

Emily laughed. "I don't know if this is what they mean."

Her father only shrugged his shoulders.

A knock sounded at the door and both her and her father looked at her mother.

"Are you expecting someone?" he asked.

Her mother stood up and began to make her way to the door. Both Emily and her father followed after her as she began to talk.

"Remember how I said I took care of the house? Well, Lord Brimsby was terribly upset when you didn't make it to dinner. Went on about how long the travels were and how he doesn't even lodge in London often. I told him that I was looking at getting rid of this place and he offered to take it off my hands. He said he was coming by this morning to sign the papers."

Mrs. Underwood opened the door to reveal an older man, most likely just a few years younger than her mother, dressed in a tight black suit and a tall top hat. "Good morning, Mrs. Underwood. I suspect that everything is in order? I don't have much time so invite me in and throw on a pot of tea."

Emily's brows furrowed and she grimaced at how he ordered her mother around.

Her father took a step forward, placing his arm around her mother's shoulders. "Afraid we don't have time for tea. Not to worry though, we can sign the papers right here in the entry."

Lord Brimsby scoffed. "And who might you be?"

"This is my husband, Angus, I believe I mentioned him in our prior meetings."

"Not a widow after all then," he said, his voice trailing off. "And your daughter? Has she come to her senses yet?"

Emily stepped into the hallway. She leaned against the wall, crossing her arms over her chest. "She has."

Lord Brimsby looked up at Emily and his face began to twist in anger. "You!" he yelled as he pushed his way into the house, nearly shoving her father to the side. "How *dare* you show your face after standing me up like that. Do you know who I am?"

"Unfortunately, yes. And might I say, your reputation precedes you."

"You should be grateful I even gave you the time of day!" he exclaimed, straightening himself and running his hands down his suit. His voice evened out but somehow, it still reminded her of a toddler not getting his way. "Now, If you beg for my forgiveness, I might be gracious enough to give you a second chance."

Emily laughed. "Beg you for a second chance? You are even more vile than I thought. I have no intention of marrying you or *begging* you for anything. In fact, you must excuse me. I have a very important appointment to attend."

Emily walked around a now red-faced lord. As she turned from him completely he tried to follow her, hurling one final insult.

"You pretentious little bitch," he spat, "and here I was doing charity work for your widowed mother."

Her father pushed Emily behind him towards her mother and took a calm step forward. "I apologize for my daughter. She clearly still has a lot to learn," he said as the lord turned his attention to him. "What she meant to say was—" faster than Emily could see, her father's fist connected with Lord Brimsby's jawline, sending him flying backwards onto the hard wooden floor.

"Oh my god!" her mother shrieked as her father shook out his fist.

He turned away from the bloody lord on the ground with a calm smile. "Oh right, I did leave one thing out. I can now throw one hell of a punch."

He reached forward and held the door open, extending his other arm in a mocking bow.

"To new adventures," he said in a cheery tone.

Emily curtsied as she walked out the doorway followed by both her parents. Shuffling sounded from behind them and as she turned her head to look over her shoulder, Emily could see Lord Brimsby now leaning against the door frame, cupping the side of his face.

"What do you think you are doing walking away from me?!"

"Well, would you believe me if I said I had a pirate to find?"

He looked at her as if she were daft. "...No?"

"Well, that's a shame then. You would do well with a little imagination."

She gave him her back as she and grabbed both of her parents' hands and led them back to the library where her own story truly started.

She had to have hope that he was alive. He was Flynn Sawyer, dastardly pirate thief who overthrows the king and leads a revolt.

His story does not end in tragedy.

Now, dear reader, I must say that as Emily walked through town under the warmth of the morning sun, elated at her own decision to go back, finally freeing herself from her previous life, she should have noted the calmness of the weather around them. Then again, weather is such a fickle thing. You never know when a storm is around the corner, and don't you know, incredible things can happen in a storm.

Good incredible things.

But I know you are eager for the ending, so, lets get back to the story.

As they approached the library, Emily's happiness began to dissipate as she looked at the 'Closed' sign on the front door. But more than that, the building looked...different. It had always looked old, but this time the library looked truly abandoned. Like it had been ignored for hundreds of years. The sign itself was covered in a thick layer of dust and the very bricks of the building were now cracked.

"What happened?" Emily mumbled.

"Time," Ms. Lewis said from behind them. They all turned around to see the librarian standing just a few feet behind them, holding an open umbrella over her head. "Time is such a pesky thing, though, nothing some hard work and luck won't fix."

"Are you...leaving?" Emily asked.

Ms. Lewis shrugged her shoulders. "Isn't that what you're doing? Finding somewhere new?" Her voice was calm, endearing even.

"I suppose so, but I left something here and I really need to find it."

Ms. Lewis smiled. "I left it in the Green Room for you, right on the table. Oh, but do hurry." She tipped her umbrella back so she could look at the sky above them. "It seems like the perfect morning for a storm."

Emily's mother looked at her with furrowed brows. "It's been clear skies all morning?"

But as the words left her mother's mouth, the skies above them darkened and rain began to pour down, drenching them in seconds. Emily raced for the handle and threw the door open. They all rushed inside and as Emily turned to hold the door for Ms. Lewis, she looked out onto the street just to discover that she was gone.

"Close the door!" her mother yelled.

Emily did as she was told, causing the bell above it to jingle.

"It's right at the very back!" she said as she started running towards the Green Room.

Please work.

She opened the door to the hidden room, rushing in, with her parents following behind her. The book was exactly where Ms. Lewis said, already opened to the ending.

The family walked over to the table and stood around it, staring down at the final page.

"What now?" her mother asked, looking at her father.

"Don't ask me," he said. "It's Emily's book."

Emily leaned down, reaching for the book. "Maybe we have to—"

The windows burst open, a crack of lightning illuminating the room. As quickly as it appeared, Emily and her parents vanished. The wind ceased abruptly, causing the windows to slam shut. Only the book remained in that empty broken down library that never once had a visitor outside of Emily herself.

And with time, it too would fade away.

REGRETS

Flynn

Flynn woke up to the light streaming through an open window and a hot pain radiating from his abdomen. He groaned as he sat up, trying to ignore the pulling and tearing sensation as he swung his feet over the bed frame.

He flicked off the covers of the bed and looked down at the white bandage tightly wrapped around his waist, stained with small spots of pink where he had been shot.

The memories came flooding back.

He looked around him and his heart fell. He was back at his mother's inn. Emily was gone, and he felt like it was his heart that had been shot.

The door to his room opened and he looked up as his mother walked in, carrying a tray of warm bread, fish, and black coffee. She kicked the door closed behind her, paying him no mind, as she walked across the room to the desk, setting the food down.

"You have been sleeping for three days," she said calmly

as she fiddled with the utensils, straightening them out. "How do you feel?"

Flynn watched his mother as he sat on the edge of the bed. When she was loud and yelling, Flynn could handle it, though, when she got quiet, that is when Flynn knew that she was truly cross.

"Good," he mumbled. "I'll be fine."

She released a breath as she turned around. Flynn's heart felt wracked with guilt as he looked at her. She looked just as she did when his father died. Her eyes looked exhausted and her face appeared to have aged with worry.

She walked over to the bed and sat down beside him.

"What happened out there?" she asked. "Levi and Lucas, they were on about everything, but we are all just as confused as one another. Where is Emily?"

Flynn hesitated. "She's gone. I sent her home..." He looked down at his mother who was watching him patiently. "She isn't from our world," he finally blurted out. He needed to explain everything. "As crazy as it sounds, she appeared on the streets the night I went to Oakden. First there was a few strikes of lightening. When as they disappeared, I saw her in the streets. Everything about her was odd and different, but at the same time, I felt like I knew her for an eternity. She told me that she was from a place called London. As the weeks went on, I couldn't bring myself to let her go home. I wanted to keep her here." He looked at his mother again and she was still listening intently. He sighed as he continued, "But when I got shot, I realized it very well could have been her in my stead, so when the light to her world appeared again I sent her home. I know I did the right thing, but I hate myself for it."

His mother nodded her head, seeming to take everything in, but rather than the litany of questions he was expecting, she only asked one.

"Did you do the right thing?"

"Of course I did. Keeping her here would have been selfish."

"Did you ask her, Flynn? Did you ask her if she wanted to go home where it was safe or stay here, in our world, with us? With *you*?"

Flynn hesitated. "I didn't need to. I was protecting her—"

"You were protecting yourself," she scolded. "I know love can be scary. Heavens knows how often your father scared me, but you will never find happiness if you aren't willing to take a risk and be selfish once in a while."

Flynn shook his head, fighting away the wetness that threatened to form in his eyes "So what am I supposed to do then?"

His mother sighed as she stood up from the bed, evening out her dress with her hands.

"There is nothing you can do. You made sure of that yourself." She walked towards the door, but she paused long enough to add one more dose of guilt to the already growing pile. "I love you, my boy, but sometimes, you are too much like your father."

FLYNN SAT at the tavern downing another mug of ale. He had been up on his feet for over a week now, but the pain in his heart only grew with each day that passed.

Each night, he lay awake in his bed wondering what Emily was doing. He tried convincing himself that he made the right choice. She would marry a man with more money than what Flynn had stolen. Money that was probably earned. Perhaps she would even have children and live a quiet life—a life he could never provide. But each reason he came up with only felt like a bitter lie. And the thought of her marrying someone else only made his anger and despair root deeper within his heart.

Flynn began to lift his mug again, but a hand came down on the top of the cup before swiping it away.

He looked up to Levi who was staring down at him with a hardened expression.

"What do you think you're doing?" Flynn asked.

"I could ask you the same thing. You've been coming here since you woke up. We need to make a plan. Lucas is waiting in the Captain's Cabin. Let's go." Levi set the mug down on the other end of the bar as he began to walk out.

Flynn scoffed. "A plan for what?"

Levi stopped and let out a deep breath as he slowly turned around and walked back to Flynn. "I know you're hurting," Levi began, "but we have all lost people. You need to get over yourself. At least my sister is still out there some-where. Emily isn't special. She is gone. She is not coming back. Ever."

Flynn stood up from his chair and took a step forward. "You may be my friend, but I would advise that you keep her name out of your mouth."

Levi narrowed his eyes. "Or what? You'll send me away as well? Well, you're doing a fine job of it already. This is important. We need to find my sister. That was the deal when you recruited me. Help me get her back, not wallow about some woman who is probably already bedding her new husband—"

Flynn tackled Levi to the ground and they began to fight. Flynn ignored the pain in his abdomen as he landed a punch on Levi's jaw. Levi managed to get a few shots in as they each struggled to pin the other down. The bar doors slammed open and within seconds Levi was pulled away, leaving Flynn flat on his back, panting.

Lucas stepped in between them, his one good eye angrily darting between them. "You both need to pull your heads out of your asses. Levi, go take a walk."

Levi spat on the bar floor as he pushed himself to his feet and stormed out of the tavern. Lucas walked over to Flynn and grabbed his hand, helping him to his feet. He tried to hide his wince as his muscles moved to help him stand.

They both walked back over to the bar and took a seat.

Usually, Flynn was the one dealing with Lucas and Levi. It almost felt embarrassing letting his emotions get the better of him.

"Cap," Lucas began, "you need to let her go. She would want you to live your life. Not rot away here, pushing everyone away."

Flynn didn't respond right away. "I don't know how to forget her," he eventually said. "There is not a thing I could do from this point on that would be without her influence. It is like she melded herself to every part of me, always there, reminding me of the happy ending that was not meant for me. Sometimes I think I even see her, but when I blink, she is gone."

Lucas patted Flynn's back. "You know I am here for you, but Levi is right to be angry. You sent her away, and we do not know that she will ever return. But his sister is out there. We need to look for her."

"You help him," Flynn said as he leaned back in his chair. "I want to help, I want to search, but I cannot leave. Not when we only just killed the king. My focus needs to be here where I can still monitor the movements of the Emerald Guard. Levi will forgive me with time. Let him be angry. It will only fuel him."

Lucas bit his bottom lip as he shook his head. "Or, it will push him away."

HELLO, AGAIN

DARDURIN, 1730, TWO WEEKS AFTER THE MASQUERADE

Emily

Emily opened her eyes and rather than the cobblestone ground of Oakden, she stared down at a sandy beach. She looked to her side and saw both of her parents start to stand up, looking as confused as she was that first night she arrived.

"Impossible," her mother said.

"Improbable," Emily corrected as she laughed.

Emily stood up and brushed the sand off of her dress. When she looked up, she saw Martha's inn.

"It worked," she whispered to herself.

Emily left her parents on the beach as she began sprinting through the sand towards the town. All the memories she had created with Flynn came flooding to the front of her mind at full force. There was not a doubt in her head that this was where she was meant to be. The only thing missing? Her pirate.

She stopped outside of the door to the inn, her heart

pounding wildly against her chest. She took a deep breath and opened the door.

She stepped inside of the inn. Martha looked up from her desk and when she met Emily's gaze, her eyes widened and she jumped to her feet, rushing towards Emily.

"Emily! Oh, thank heavens you are back!" she yelled as she reached for Emily's hands, holding them tight in her own. "How is this possible? Flynn told us everything, he told us about who you are."

At the sound of Flynn's name, Emily's heart picked up pace. "Is Flynn hurt?"

Martha shook her head. "He's been better, but he seems more broken by your absence than he does from the gun shot."

"Where is he?" she asked with urgency in her voice.

"I'm sure Lucas and Levi will know. Besides, they've been missing you as well. Though they might not admit it," she said with a wink. "They are at the tavern. Go on now. We've all waited long enough for you to come home to us."

Emily smiled as she dropped Martha's hands and turned on her heels and rushed to the door. As she opened the door again and stepped out into the street, she stopped, turning her head to look over her shoulder.

"By the way," she began, "I brought a few people with me. They are still down at the beach. Please make them feel at home."

"Always, dear," Martha said with a warm smile.

Emily turned back and ran down the street towards the tavern. She finally knew what she wanted. She only hoped he wanted her, too.

Emily threw open the tavern door to see Mr. Balks behind the bar cleaning out a mug, Levi already half drunk and miserable looking, leaned with his back against the bar and Lucas beside him. Everyone turned their heads to see Emily.

Levi nearly spit out his drink when he saw her. He started coughing as he set his ale down. "What the fuck," he said through coughs.

Lucas stood up and carefully walked over to Emily. His gaze was cold and she couldn't make out any of what he might have been feeling. "You lied to us," he said. Emily swallowed nothing as she prepared herself to apologize, but his expression melted into one of warmth as the slightest smile appeared. "You're a better pirate than I thought."

Emily released her held breath and laughed, jumping forward to pull him into a hug.

"Damn," Levi said as he walked over to her. "I just finished telling your bastard to get over you. Ha," he said with an empty laugh. "Who knew getting rid of a princess would be so hard." He walked past them, patting her head twice before he left. "Glad you're back."

Emily watched as he left and turned back to look at Lucas who seemed to mirror Levi's sadness as he watched his friend.

"What's wrong with him?"

Lucas sighed as he looked down at Emily. "We haven't found any leads on his sister. And with the recent usurp, Flynn will be busy with keeping an eye on the Emerald Guard making sure they don't appoint someone to the throne who would become like the late king. So, he can't come with Levi to look for his sister. He is broken right now."

Emily's heart fell.

How could I forget?

"Will you go with him?"

Lucas chuckled as he stepped back from Emily. "Of

course. Someone has to keep him safe. More importantly, I'm guessing you came back for more than just this beautiful mug?"

She smiled, brushing her hair behind her ear. "Where is he?"

~

EMILY WALKED across the deck of Flynn's ship. She ran her hands along the rails, feeling every groove and crack in the wood.

I'm finally back.

She bit back a smile as she walked towards the helm, stopping when she saw him. Flynn was leaning against the helm, looking out at the ocean in front of him, his back to her.

Whatever butterflies she swallowed felt as though they had multiplied ten-fold as she took another careful step towards him.

"I don't want to hear it, Lucas," Flynn said, not turning around.

She took a deep breath and steadied her voice.

"Pirate," she said, unable to hold back her smile.

Flynn slowly turned his head over his shoulders, and when he saw her, it looked as if life was breathed back into his eyes. He still did not move, instead he watched as she walked up to him. She looked down at his waist where a white bandage was tightly wrapped. She took a final step up to him and reached her hand out to touch it. But before she could, his hand shot out and grabbed her wrist.

She glanced up at him and he looked like he didn't believe that she was here.

"How?" he whispered as his eyes searched hers.

"Well, I needed to return this," she said as she reached into her pocket and pulled out his compass. She moved her wrist so that she could place the compass in his open hand and close her hands over top of his. "My whole life I felt as if I were wandering, never truly having any sense of direction. But really, all of the choices I have made in my life have led me here, to you. I...I love—"

Flynn cut off her words with a desperate kiss. He dropped her hands and grabbed her waist, pulling her closer. She melted into his touch as a warmth she never knew she could claim as her own washed over her heart.

He pulled away from her, pressing his forehead against hers. "I love you, Princess. But, now that I have you back, I don't think I will ever be able to send you away again."

"Then don't. I want to experience everything together, Pirate."

Flynn stood up fully, brushing her hair out of her face as he watched her with a kindness in his eyes that was meant for only her.

"What would you like to do first? Name anything."

Emily thought of all the books she had read so far. All the sappy happily ever afters and over the top confessions of love. She once thought that they were a thing of fairy tales and fiction. But now, she understood how someone could lose themselves in their partners eyes.

"Would it be too much to sail under the setting sun?"

Flynn shook his head gently. "You are mine, Princess. Mine to heal, mine to serve, mine to protect, and above all else, *mine to love*. Whatever you ask, it will never be too much."

EPILOGUE

THREE MONTHS LATER, DARDURIN

Emily

"Are you sure you can't come with us?" Lucas asked as he loaded the final crate onto Flynn's old ship.

Flynn dusted off his hands as he walked up to Emily, placing his large hand gently on her waist. She looked up at him and that same kind but possessive look danced across his eyes.

"We will be taking a break from the adventures for a while," Flynn said, looking back at Lucas. "Besides, we need to keep an eye on the Emerald Guard. They will be looking to appoint someone soon. We are needed here."

"But," Emily chimed in, "we will be waiting for your return. With *her*. I already have a room ready in the inn."

Lucas nodded his head as he looked back at the Helm where Levi was instructing some of the crew members from her father's old fleet.

It had been three months, but Levi had refused to say more than three words to Flynn.

"We both thank you, Emily," Lucas said with a shy smile.

They helped with the final touches and as the tide began to grow, they watched from the port as their friend's ship sailed off.

A lot had happened in the three short months since her return. The main being her own relationship with her pirate.

"So, Mrs. Sawyer," Flynn said from behind her as he placed gentle kisses on her neck. "What is Pip saying? Will we have an easy night or is she angry with me as well?"

Emily turned her head to look at Flynn as he dropped his hand to her stomach. "You're so sure it's a girl?"

"Yes, and she will be just as beautiful and just as cunning as her mother. When your parents return, we will tell them. *Together.*"

"My mother will knit enough blankets to smother us," Emily said through her own smile.

Mrs. Underwood had acclimated to her new life among the pirates. She had left Dardurin to go sailing with Mr. Underwood. And with a clean-shaven face and his old name, he was able to let go of Blood Beard and live a quiet and peaceful life, alongside his wife.

Mr. Balks still spent each day fishing and telling stories of how the evil king was overthrown.

Martha's inn was busy enough with all of *Blood Beard's* old crew members who decided to stay. Now, she usually didn't have more than one spare room at a time.

Levi still held anger towards Flynn, but more than anything, he recently found the first clue to tracking down his sister. Lucas had stuck close by his side since Emily's return, that even she began to notice the glint in his eyes as he looked at Levi.

"I wonder what will happen with the two of them in charge of their own crew," Emily pondered as she looked out at the ship, disappearing into the horizon.

"Probably nothing good," Flynn answered.

As for Emily and Flynn, well let's just say that their happily ever after didn't end with just a kiss. It blossomed into their own story, finally getting that second book they had promised each other.

A GOODBYE FOR NOW

Oh don't be too upset now. After all, all stories must eventually come to an end.

Do not worry. I will be back soon enough with a new story of adventure, capture, daring escapes, and true love, when the time is right.

I myself have never been the best at goodbyes. Why, even now, as I pack up my books and ready myself for the next adventure, I find myself trying to find the right words. If I were to leave you with a message, a moral of our story today if you will, I would say have some imagination. The world is just so incredibly boring without it.

Now, I really must be going. Even as I step out into the streets, the rain starts to pour down on me. I smile, looking up at the darkening sky. The beginnings of *quite* the storm.

"You think you're so clever, don't you," I say to the other storytellers waiting for my return as I step out into the bustling streets of London, England, 1852.

I suppose, I should at the very least tell you my name before I go. I have had many names assigned to me over the years. But I think that my most recent one is perhaps my favorite. After all, Ms. Lewis has a nice ring to it. Don't you agree, dear reader?

-L

SNEAK PEEK: HIS TO HEAL

TWO MONTHS AFTER EMILY'S RETURN

Lucas

Every story has a beginning. But not all beginnings are simple or straightforward. In fact, I find that *most* beginnings are rather messy.

Lucas leaned against the doorframe of the tavern that had been closed for the last several hours, watching Levi sit quietly at the bar. A few empty mugs sat abandoned around him.

He wasn't drinking, at least not anymore. He wasn't laughing or smiling. He seemed like a shell of himself.

Lucas took a step into the room causing Levi to look up. "We will find her, Levi. I swear it. We will bring her home."

Levi looked at him, his eyes darkening as he stood up and took slow purposeful steps towards Lucas. Only stopping when there was just a breath of space between them. "Why do you want to help?"

"You're drunk, Levi. But even still, you know I am your... friend." The words stung because they were the ultimate truth, and yet, Lucas still felt like he was lying. "You do not need to always suffer alone. You can rely on others, too."

Levi scoffed. "My friend?" He ran his hand through his messy hair, pushing it back out of his face. "You can hardly stand me."

"What about you then?" Lucas asked. "Do you not think of me as your friend after everything we have been through? Have faith in me. I promise, even if it's the last thing I do, we will get Ada back."

WHILE YOU WAIT

If you have time, dear reader, please leave
a review!
Check out my Patreon for bonus content!

<u>Out now</u>

A Crown of Aconite

Dancing with the Headless Horseman

<u>**Coming soon**</u>

His To Heal, Second Chance Books 2

A Crown of Lycoris, Aconite Series

AUTHOR NOTE

I love being able to share my stories with you, and as any author does, I hope that you can find enjoyment in these worlds and characters.

Writing this book was so much fun! I have always been fascinated with pirates, so being able to bring this book to life was an amazing experience.

To stay up to date on what's going on with new works, check out my socials or subscribe to my monthly newsletter!

instagram.com/author_elenahcovens

tiktok.com/@author_elenahcovens

ACKNOWLEDGMENTS

First I always must thank my family for their support in this writing journey.

I also have to thank the support of this little book community that we are growing, I would not be here without you. I would just be the neighbourhood crazy lady talking about pirates and fantasy and all of those wonderfully crazy things.

Ana and Reese, thank you for staying up with me to edit this chaos until 4am, *multiple*, nights in a row. You guys are insane but I couldn't ask for more supportive friends. I love you guys. <3

To my PA, Tanisha, you are—as always—a life saver!

And to my friends, its way too late to leave me now. We are in this together. :)